Lady Rample

and the Mysterious Mr. Singh

Lady Rample Mysteries – Book Seven

Shéa MacLeod

Shéa MacLeod

Chapter 1

"M'lady?" My maid, Maddie, popped her head through the doorway of my study. Her mob cap was slightly askew, and there was a smudge of flour on her cheek.

Oh, dear. That could only mean one thing. She'd attempted to bake something again.

Ever since she'd found May Byron's *Cake Book* in my library—I'd oddly no recollection of how it got there—she'd become obsessed with baking. Unfortunately, her enthusiasm far outmatched her abilities. Her skills mostly ran to tea and toast with the occasional sandwich thrown in for good measure. This was a pity, as I did so love cake.

I sniffed the air subtly, but I didn't catch the distinctive scorched odor I'd become so familiar with. Either she'd managed to pull it off at last, or it had yet to go in the oven.

"What is it, Maddie?" I turned back to my desk where I was going through an enormous pile of correspondence. I'd gotten a bit behind thanks to the return of my paramour, Hale Davis. But as he was currently practicing with his band—Hale is a marvelous jazz musician and a wiz on the ivories—I was trying desperately to get caught up. In fact, I was in the middle of answering a letter from a new friend of mine, Phil, who happened to be the cousin of my own cousin-by-marriage, Binky.

I'd met Phil quite by accident while on a mission at the great shopping mecca, Harrods. Binky had been showing her the town and I'd all but invited myself to join them for luncheon. Phil and I had hit it off immediately, and while she lived in an adorable mews house in London not far from my own home, I liked to keep up a regular correspondence.

"There's a gentleman to see you." Maddie fidgeted, shifting her weight from one foot to the other.

"I'm not expecting anyone. If it's Chaz, tell him to help himself to the liquor cabinet—not that he needs any encouragement—and I'll be there in two ticks." My best friend, Charles "Chaz" Raynott, frequently dropped by for no other reason than a cocktail and a chinwag.

"Er, no m'lady, it isn't Mr. Chaz. And I've put him in the kitchen."

I dropped my pen with a clatter. Ink splotted on a partially finished missive. Devil take it. "The *kitchen*? One does not put guests in the kitchen, Maddie."

"Yes, I know m'lady. And I wouldn't usually except... well, he insisted." She shrugged her bony shoulders and gave me an apologetic look.

That was beyond unusual. Gentlemen didn't insist on being seen in the kitchen. That was for workers and lower-class types. Not that I wouldn't invite them into my parlor. I don't much hold with the whole upstairs-downstairs nonsense. I may be the wealthy Ophelia, Lady Rample, widow of Lord Rample now, but once upon a time I grew up in a small village amongst ordinary people. And while I do not consider myself ordinary by any stretch, I most *definitely* do not consider myself above anyone simply because of a lucky turn of the wheel of life, so to speak.

"Who *is* it, Maddie?" I demanded, finally having enough of her dithering.

"It's Mr. Singh himself," she said in barely a whisper. Maddie was somewhat in awe of Mr. Singh. Frankly, I didn't blame her.

"Why didn't you say so?" I rescued my pen and laid it in its box. "I will see him immediately. I don't suppose your latest experiment turned out? Cake with tea would be lovely."

"'Fraid not," she admitted, leading the way downstairs. "I forgot to turn on the oven."

"Of course you did." I sighed. Maddie was a decent maid but a dreadful cook. "Have you turned it on now?"

"Yes, but it's only been ten minutes. I… don't think it'll be ready." She frowned as if unsure if that were true or not.

"You're probably right. It should, however, be ready sooner than three hours." That was the most recent incident. I'd no idea what had gone into the over, but the thing had been a brick of charcoal when it came out.

Maddie sniffed. "I think I can manage to get it out on time."

I nearly said something very sarcastic but then decided better of it. If Maddie ever did manage to conquer this baking thing, I wanted to eat her cakes, not be poisoned by them. "I've no doubt you can. I'm looking forward to trying it." I just hoped it was edible.

I stepped into the kitchen. My aunt's Sikh butler sat at the table, hands neatly folded, dressed in his usual black suit. "Mr. Singh! Is everything alright? Has something happened to my aunt?"

He stood up, his pink *dastar* nearly brushing the low ceiling. "My lady." He bowed slightly and with great gravity. "Your aunt is well. I am sorry to have alarmed you, but I am here on a personal matter."

What an astonishing turn of events! "A personal matter?"

"I have a great favor to ask."

Well, that was unusual. Mr. Singh could always be relied upon in times of crisis, but he'd never once required my help or, as far as I knew, anyone else's. "Perhaps we should go somewhere more private?"

He shook his head. "This is good enough for me, my lady. And I'm certain Miss Maddie will keep what she hears to herself." The look he gave Maddie made her go pale. She may have even let out a squeak.

"Mum's the word," she said, although not particularly cheerfully. "May Jehovah strike me dead if I talk."

"Well, that's a bit dramatic," I murmured. To Mr. Singh I said, "Sit down." I took the chair across from him. "Maddie, tea please. And some biscuits if there are any."

"There's some custard creams," she said, bustling over to the stove.

"Perfect."

Despite Maddie's assurances of keeping her mouth shut, we waited until she'd finished making tea and left the room. I'd no doubt she was eavesdropping, but at least we'd the appearance of privacy.

"Now, Mr. Singh. How can I help you?" I couldn't imagine what this favor could be. After all, Mr. Singh was one of the most capable people I knew. Him needing anyone's help seemed completely out of character.

He eyed me carefully, and it was as if his dark brown eyes could see straight into my soul. It was a tad uncomfortable while being oddly comforting at the same time. Mr. Singh was not someone to be easily fooled, and there was a sort of security in that.

"This morning," he said at last, "I received a letter from an old friend."

"Well, that's nice," I said a bit lamely. I'd no idea what else to say. Letters from old friends are nice, but not exactly earth-shattering. And I still couldn't figure out what it had to do with me.

"The thing is, my lady, this friend died."

"Oh, I'm sorry. What terrible news."

"No, my lady, you misunderstand." He leaned forward. "She died many years ago, yet the letter arrived only this morning."

Now that *was* curious. "How dashed odd."

He eased back. "Indeed."

"Perhaps she's not dead? If she's writing letters, I mean."

"She is most definitely dead. This letter was postmarked many years ago."

That cleared things up a bit. "So the letter got lost in the post. Isn't that a matter for the Royal Mail? I don't see how I could possibly help."

He tilted his head slightly to the right. "Did you know that I served during the war?"

He meant the Great War, of course. I hadn't known, but it didn't come as a surprise. He was of the right age, and many men from India had fought on behalf of the Empire. It would certainly explain certain skills he possessed. "I did not."

"I was injured and sent to the hospital in Brighton to recover."

I realized he referred to the Royal Pavilion. Built as a pleasure palace for King George IV, the former royal residence had been turned into a hospital for Indian Corps troops injured on the Western Front. It was believed the place, which had all the appearance of a palace transported directly from India itself, would make the men feel more at home. I was both astonished and unsurprised that Mr. Singh had spent time there.

"I'm very sorry to hear that, but I'm very glad you survived the war."

"As I am glad you survived," he said softly.

I'd been a nursing aide during the war. Doing my part and all that. I'd seen and done things that sometimes still haunted my nightmares, but I preferred not to think of them and to put them behind me like a bad dream. I suppose it was my way of dealing with the trauma of it all.

"While I was recovering," he continued, "I met a young nurse. An Englishwoman. Her name was Emily Pearson. We struck up a friendship. She made my days much… brighter."

There was something in his voice, his eyes. I wondered just how close this friendship had been. I was betting closer than a handshake. "Go on."

"When word came that I would be released and sent back to the Front, we planned to meet in secret the night before. I waited for hours, but she never arrived. The next day, before I left, I asked one of the other nurses about her. She told me Emily had disappeared the day before. Her bed hadn't been slept in. No one had heard from her. I wanted to stay, but I had no choice. I was shipped back to France that very day."

I wondered if, perhaps, Emily had gone without leave. It happened sometimes. Facing so many injured and dying soldiers, so much horror day after day... it became too much for some. "How did you find out what happened to her?"

He nodded, his expression grave. "Her friend Dorothy, the one to whom I'd spoken. She wrote me. Included a clipping of a newspaper." He pulled a folded bit of paper out of his pocked and slid it across the table to me.

It had obviously been read many times as it was fragile and heavily creased. I unfolded it carefully and spread it on the table. The letter was in neat, feminine handwriting. It had an address in Brighton and the words "I'm sorry." It was signed Dorothy Evans. The other was a small newspaper article about a dead body fished out of the pond at Queens Park. The body of a young nurse who'd gone missing a week before. Suicide, it said.

My sorrow over the wasted life of this young nurse, and the feelings Mr. Singh must have had for her to keep these things so long, made my throat thick and my eyes sting. I folded the letter back up very neatly and handed it back. There were so many things I didn't know about the mysterious Mr. Singh. "I'm so sorry."

He nodded. "Thank you. At the time it was a shock. But I thought nothing more of it."

"You weren't surprised she killed herself?"

He cocked his head thoughtfully. "Yes and no. She hadn't seemed in that state of mind, but then with everything going on—"

I knew what he meant. So much tragedy. Sometimes it snuck up on a person. "I still don't see how I can help."

He took a second letter from his pocket. "This arrived yesterday."

I carefully inspected the envelope. The stamp was old, the postmark from 1914. The address was to him at his former regiment but had clearly been rerouted recently. Either Royal Mail had lost the letter, or the regiment had. In either case, a nearly twenty-year-old letter had finally found its way home.

"Read it," he urged.

I unfolded it. Though the paper was old and stained, it wasn't nearly as worn as the first letter had been. I squinted at the badly smudged ink inside, struggling to make out the words. "Dear Chehzaad." I glanced up at Mr. Singh. I'd never known his first name.

"It means 'a young prince.' My mother had very grand ideas," he said dryly. "Go on."

"I am writing you because I must tell someone, and I know I can trust you. I can trust you, can't I? I'm certain I can. I don't know who else to turn to. You see, I have found something out. Something quite terrible, and I fear my life is in danger. If they knew, they would kill me. They've done such terrible—" A large smear blotted out whatever she'd meant to say. "I need proof. No one will believe me if I don't have it. I'm going—" The rest of the letter was completely obliterated. At some point it had gotten damp and the ink had smeared beyond all recognition. "Well, she was definitely frightened."

"I agree. I no longer believe she killed herself."

"What do you think happened?" I asked, handing him back the letter.

"I believe that whatever it was Emily found out put her life in danger. That she did not leave that night willingly but was dragged away by whomever she was afraid of. And I believe they murdered her."

It made a sort of sense. "Why bring this to me?"

"Because you were a nurse. You know what her life was like. More, you have a keen investigative mind, as we have discovered recently, and many important connections.

I need your help to find out who did this to Emily and why and to bring them to justice."

Trying to solve a mystery from almost twenty years ago would be a challenge the likes of which I'd never faced before. My biggest yet. Still, I didn't even have to think about it. "Justice for Emily. What's the plan?"

Just then, the kitchen door banged inward, and in strode my aunt. She paused elegantly on the threshold, struck a dramatic pose in her equally dramatic aubergine dress and matching cloche, and eyed us both from beneath exotically painted eyelids.

"Aunt Butty?" I said.

"Tell me quickly," she said. "Who died?"

Chapter 2

"What are you doing here?" I said instead of answering Aunt Butty's question.

My aunt took a seat next to me and helped herself to a custard cream. Somehow she managed to get crumbs on her ample bosom before she'd even taken a bite. Stray curls gone silver peeked from beneath the cloche which she hadn't removed. Too bad because every time she turned her head, she whapped me in the face with the giant mustard-colored ostrich feather poking out from the side.

"I am here, my dear, because the two of you," she gave Mr. Singh the stink eye, "are in clear need of my help."

She took an enormous bite of her biscuit and chewed furiously.

"What makes you say that?" I said dryly.

She helped herself to tea, took a deep sip, then let out a gusty sigh. "You always need my help."

Which wasn't entirely true. Although Aunt Butty's help was often appreciated, it could be a bit... overwhelming and unnecessary. Take, for instance, the fact that she rescued me from the vicarage where I grew up. I was sixteen and desperate to get away from a domineering father and a small-minded village. Her help then was both entirely appropriate and immensely gratifying. Take, however, the day she decided I needed help with my wardrobe. The resulting shock to the senses left me reeling for weeks. I'd had to replace most of it quietly and at great expense. One simply does not need or desire half a dozen silk kaftans in lime with maroon stitching. Nor does one require the matching turbans to go with them. Not at my age—nor at any age—I'm quite certain.

"Beside which, I overheard Mr. Singh talking on the telephone this morning about *murder*. I didn't get all the details, but you must know it piqued my interest. Very juicy. Tell me everything."

"You were eavesdropping, my lady?" Mr. Singh's tone was stiff. If he hadn't been so in control of his expressions, he no doubt would have been radiating outrage.

She waved airily. "Not intentionally, of course, but the walls are *très* thin, you know."

"Who else did you tell?" I asked Mr. Singh in an attempt to prevent any hard feelings between Mr. Singh and my aunt.

"I was speaking with an old army mate. He was also in Brighton. I wanted to know what he remembered."

"And did he remember anything useful?"

Before Mr. Singh could answer, Aunt Butty let out a huff. "Do clue a girl in, will you?"

I rolled my eyes and gestured to Mr. Singh. "It's your story."

He was quiet a moment, then slowly and briefly relayed the story of Emily to Aunt Butty. By the time he finished, my aunt was dabbing her eyes with a white linen handkerchief she'd pulled out of her bosom.

"Oh, that is simply dreadful. That poor girl. What do you suppose she found out that put her in such danger?" She took a fortifying sip of tea.

"I do not know," Mr. Singh admitted. "But, as I was about to tell my lady," he nodded to me, "I spoke with a friend I served with. He was shot in the leg and sent to the Pavilion to recuperate. He knew Emily also."

"What did he say?" I asked, helping myself to another custard cream.

"He remembered her disappearance and what came after. He remained for a couple of weeks after I left. He, too, thought it odd her death would be ruled a suicide. Even stranger, he said that right before she disappeared, two men in officers' uniforms arrived at the hospital. They were there only briefly, but Emily seemed frightened of them. After she disappeared, they came again and went through her things."

"Well, that's dashed odd," I said. "I wonder why they did that. Looking for something, I'll bet. Evidence perhaps? Did your friend know who they were?"

"He assumed they were with the investigative branch and were trying to help locate her. He remarked that one had a scar on his face as if from shrapnel."

"Makes sense," Aunt Butty said around a mouthful off custard cream. "Who else would they bring in?"

"The police," I said dryly. "That's who usually investigates deaths."

"The military prefers not to have the local constabulary involved in its business," Mr. Singh reminded me. "I'm certain if they could avoid bringing in the locals, they would have done so."

"How daft of them. That's what the police are good at. Solving crimes. Well, most of them anyway." There were a few who could use a good course in detective work. Although North, the detective chief inspector I often found myself tangling with, was turning out not to be such a bad fellow.

"So where do we start?" Aunt Butty asked.

"A very good question. Mr. Singh?" After all, this was his investigation. His friend who'd been murdered.

He cleared his throat. "I believe these officers that arrived shortly before Emily's disappearance may have something to do with her death."

"They're certainly a good clue," Aunt Butty agreed, pouring us all more tea.

"But how to find them?" I mused. "I very much doubt we could contact the army and demand to know about two officers who visited Brighton nearly twenty years ago."

"Of course not," Aunt Butty agreed.

"What about the others who were there?" I said. "The nurses, doctors, patients. If your old army buddy remembered Emily and these men, then perhaps someone else remembers them, too."

Mr. Singh nodded. "I thought of that. We need the records of everyone who worked or stayed there, but those are kept at the War Office. It is doubtful they would give me that sort of information."

"You're right about that," I agreed. "I doubt they'd give them to me, either." I did know one person with the sort of position and power that might allow him access to such records, but I was trying to distance myself from Lord Varant now that Hale and I were officially committed to each other. It didn't seem right to keep taking advantage of Varant's connections for my investigations, even if it was for the greater good. I figured I'd keep him as a sort of ace up my sleeve. Just in case. "Where else could we get our hand on that information? What about Emily's friend, Dorothy?"

"We have her address," Mr. Singh agreed. "Or at least where she lived in Brighton during that time. Perhaps we can track her down from there."

Aunt Butty clapped her hands and let out a cackle. "Do I sense a trip coming on?"

I exchanged a glance with Mr. Singh. Then I smiled at my aunt. "Darling, pack your bags. We're off to Brighton!"

Between one thing and another, it was actually three days before we finally managed to board a train at Victoria Station bound for Brighton. In fact, we were fortunate enough to secure last minute tickets aboard the brand new electric all-Pullman service which took a mere sixty minutes station-to-station. Such a marvel!

Despite the fact that we planned to return on the very same day, Aunt Butty arrived at the station platform with Mr. Singh and a mound of luggage in tow. I myself had brought nothing but a small carryall which Hale insisted on carrying, though he wasn't coming with us. He'd a gig that night and couldn't risk being late back.

"I thought you were going for the day," he muttered, eying the no-less-than-six red-sided suitcases.

"We are." Raising my voice, I asked, "Planning to relocate, Aunt Butty?"

"One never knows when one will be forced to take shelter for the night. I have come prepared!" she declared.

She had indeed. For her ensemble matched her luggage, her cotton day dress white with red stripes, a little beribboned sailor cap perched on her silver curls, and an enormous handbag which looked like it came from the same luggage set.

"I made Mr. Singh pack, too." She pointed to a simple brown duffle which sat demurely atop her more exotic luggage.

"So I see." Poor Mr. Singh. Aunt Butty was the only person in the world who could manhandle her butler into doing whatever it was she pleased. And it wasn't simply because she paid his salary. He adored her as I did. Which was rather amusing coming from the usually stoic Mr. Singh.

Mr. Singh took charge of my bag while Hale bid me goodbye. We couldn't be terribly demonstrative in public lest it cause him trouble, but the look in his eye made me long to hurry back.

"See you tonight," he said, tone rife with meaning.

"You certainly will."

While Aunt Butty and I boarded one of the first-class cars, Mr. Singh went to oversee the loading of the luggage before taking his own seat in third class.

"I was going to pay for a seat in first," Aunt Butty said once we'd taken our seats, "but he insisted it was not his place. The man is impossible." She sat her massive handbag on the table and pulled out her latest detective novel and a pair of reading spectacles. I took the chance to have a look around at the sumptuous Art Deco interior.

We sat in a special "compartment" which was separated from the rest of the car by thin sheets of inlaid walnut wood (serving more as dividers than actual walls). The compartment held four tables draped in white cloth—two on the right of the center aisle and two on the left—on either side of which were comfortable, velvet upholstered armchairs. The floors were rubberized and covered in rich carpeting, quality art hung on the walls, and an electric heater kept the entire place cozy despite the still chilly air of early March. Essentially, it was a drawing room on wheels and quite possibly the most luxurious train I'd ever been on.

A handful of other passengers took their places in the car until it was nearly full. I recognized three of the others in our compartment. One was a well-known and somewhat scandalous stage actress. I did not recognize her male companion, though he was well-dressed with an air of grim superiority and still handsome though going gray about the temples. I imagined she was likely on her way to perform on stage in Brighton, or perhaps having a getaway with her lover.

Another of the tables was taken by two elderly spinster ladies, the Misses McGintys. They were those types of women who were comfortably neither poor nor rich, high society nor low. I'd met them via my aunt's closest friend, Louise Pennyfather. She'd had them to tea once. Distant cousins of some sort or other. A Pullman car, and one of the compartments at that, seemed a bit rich for them. But perhaps they were splurging for a special occasion. They gave me little finger waves, but otherwise seemed occupied with their own business.

A whistle blasted, and the train gave the slightest of lurches before pulling slowly out of the station. We passed through low-end neighborhoods with stained brick buildings and washing set out on lines. The sun was weak in the sky, clouds scudded overhead, but it remained dry.

Once we were out of the station, a uniformed attendant appeared as if by magic to take our breakfast order. We'd decided on an early train so as to have plenty of time in Brighton. Not to mention that the breakfast service was supposed to be phenomenal.

Over our traditional breakfasts, and fueled by plenty of both coffee and tea, Aunt Butty and I discussed our upcoming endeavors.

"Do you truly think we can obtain the records we need at the Pavilion?" I asked, slathering an inordinate amount of strawberry preserves onto a wedge of toast. "Surely they no longer have such things lying about."

"Officially, no," Aunt Butty agreed as she sliced off a piece of bacon and popped it in her mouth, chewing with gusto. "As we already discussed, those are with the War Office. However, places like the Pavilion surely have records of such things, informal as they may be. It's a town venue now, so likely there's someone there who remembers the goings on back then. Perhaps they can give us a name or two. It's the best we can do at the moment."

"Yes," I murmured. "I suppose it is. Other than learn all we can about the victim, Emily. Perhaps if we find out more about her, we can discover a key to her killer. We do need to talk to her friend, Dorothy, if we can find her."

"You think she may have told someone other than Mr. Singh about her suspicions?" Aunt Butty said around another mouthful of bacon. "This Dorothy person, perhaps?"

"Perhaps, though I fear if she did tell anyone they would have met a similar fate. Unless, of course, they kept it to themselves. There may be something of hers left, though. I supposed it would be too much to ask that she kept a diary with the name of her killer in it."

"Don't be daft, Ophelia," Aunt Butty said. "Things like that only happen in films and detective novels."

I supposed she was right, more's the pity. Why couldn't things be lovely and easy? I sighed and polished off my breakfast. Just in time, for the attendant came 'round to clear away our plates and inform us we'd be arriving at Brighton Station in a few minutes.

Unconcerned, Aunt Butty went back to reading her detective novel. I chose to look out the window and enjoy the marvelous view. Now that we were well out of London, the English countryside rolled by in never-ending waves of green dotted with little blobs of white and brown—sheep and cows, no doubt. Inky clouds roiled above.

The train slowed as it neared Brighton. Just that moment, the sky opened up and rain poured down, slashing against the windows and blurring my view. Wonderful. Brighton would no doubt prove to be a rather damp experience.

I'd been to Brighton once before as a child. My mother had been unwell, and my father had finally, rather grudgingly I thought, agreed to let her go to the seaside for some fresh air. The only reason we went to Brighton instead of somewhere else was because he'd an aunt in town who'd let us come stay with her. I remember very little about the city itself or, in fact, the seaside. What I remembered were my great-aunt's dark, dingy rooms which smelled of camphor and mothballs and burnt cabbage.

After two days, my mother insisted she was better and we should go home. My father was happy to oblige, finding such adventures a waste of time and money. I don't think Mother was better at all. More likely my great-aunt's house made her worse, and she simply longed for her own things and the fresh air of the Cotswolds countryside.

I was looking forward to creating new, more interesting memories in Brighton. Even if there was a murder involved.

At last the train lurched to a stop and everyone rose to collect their things. The Misses McGintys exited without speaking to us, so busy were they twittering about dipping their toes in the water. Weather seemed a bit frigid for that, but each to her own. The famous actress sashayed down the car, her companion close behind her. By the way he helped her down off the train, I was betting they were definitely lovers on a tryst.

Finally, Aunt Butty and I descended to the platform where Mr. Singh awaited. He bowed. "My ladies. I hope your ride was a pleasant one."

"Marvelous!" Aunt Butty sang. "I hope you were comfortable."

"Of course, madame. I have already sent the luggage on with Simon."

"Wait, Simon's here?" I asked. "And what do you mean 'sent the luggage on'?"

Simon Vale was Aunt Butty's chauffeur. We'd met him over Christmas. Aunt Butty had offered him a job. So far, I assumed he'd been satisfactory.

"I had Simon drive down earlier so we'd have a vehicle at our disposal," Aunt Butty informed me. "And naturally, I rented a hotel room just in case. Looking at the weather, I'm glad I did. At least we'll have somewhere to warm up and get dry."

"Aunt Butty, this was only supposed to be a day trip," I reminded her. In fact, that was the sole reason I'd left Maddie at home. Which I'd felt bad about. The poor girl deserved to get out in the fresh sea air. I determined that next time I'd bring her along regardless.

And then there was Hale. I'd told him I'd be returning in the evening. In fact, if all went well, I'd hoped to pop in and listen to him play for a bit.

"Well, one never knows how investigations will go. One must be prepared, Ophelia!" And with that, she sailed toward the exit.

"I suppose this means we'll have to walk to the Pavilion," I grumbled. Sending one's chauffeur ahead and then having him drive off with the luggage seemed ridiculous to me.

"Nonsense," she said. "We can hire a cab."

While we stood under the awning out of the rain, Mr. Singh flagged down a cab. Almost immediately one pulled to the curb, and Mr. Singh held the door while Aunt Butty and I climbed in the back. Then he took the front seat next to the driver.

"Where to?" the cabbie asked cheerfully. He was a plump man with small blue eyes and a fisherman's cap on his head. He smelled strongly of cheap cigars.

"Royal Pavilion," Aunt Butty said. "And step on it."

"Well, I would missus, but it's closed today." He gave her an apologetic look over his shoulder.

Well, rats. If that just didn't spoil everything.

Chapter 3

Naturally, Aunt Butty had booked a room at none
other than the Grand Hotel on the Brighton waterfront.
The glorious eight story Italianate Victorian facade shone
brilliant white even on such a gloomy day. A uniformed
doorman guarded the entrance, eyeballing any riffraff that
came too close.

Mr. Singh disappeared, no doubt to find Simon and
their own quarters. I hoped he knew what the plan was,
because I sure did not.

Inside, the hall was lined with pillars and base relief
doorways, the ceiling dripped with crystal chandeliers, and
the floor was covered in rich Aubusson carpets. A marble

staircase with ornate wrought-iron railings led gracefully to the upper floors.

We were greeted immediately by the hotel manager, who guided us to what turned out not to be a simple room, but a suite where our luggage already awaited along with a bottle of complementary champagne. I opened it immediately, pouring us both glasses, despite the fact it was barely gone ten. Didn't people drink Buck's fizz all the time? And what was that but orange juice and champagne?

"It's really too bad Louise isn't here," Aunt Butty said, referring to her dear friend. "She knows so many people in Brighton. She could easily introduce us around."

"Then why the deuce didn't you bring her?" I said. "She might have been able to send us to the right person for the information we need."

"I asked, but she refused to leave London. Peaches has been under the weather." Peaches was Louise Pennyfather's adorable ball of fluff pooch. I still felt guilty about his kidnapping during our French shenanigans. Aunt Butty tossed back her champagne and refilled her glass. "They should have given us chocolates, too, don't you think?"

"Oh, dear, I hope he'll be alright."

"Who?" Aunt Butty blinked, her thoughts obviously upon the missing chocolates.

"Peaches."

"Of course he will," she said bracingly. "She spoils that creature no end. Not to worry, I'm certain we will find what we're looking for."

I wasn't entirely certain I had Aunt Butty's confidence. Perhaps it would require a second glass of champagne.

"You know," my aunt said as we polished off the bottle, "I could really use a bite to eat. Perhaps we should start our investigation in the dining room."

"It's barely eleven, darling. Far too early for luncheon, and we just had breakfast." Although I usually didn't get up until nearly ten, my stomach informed me it was breakfast time now.

"Pish posh. Working people have elevenses all the time. I've read about it."

"We are hardly working people," I said dryly.

"But of course we are! We are working on a case." She gave me a smug look.

She had a point there. "Very well. Let us see what's on the menu."

The dining room wasn't open, but there was a lovely tea room with glass windows overlooking the sea. Potted ferns hung from every available cross beam. The walls were papered in a cream and gold bamboo pattern and the tables neatly separated by potted palms which lent the room an exotic atmosphere. Surprisingly, we were not the only residents to find our way to the tea room.

"Look at that couple in the far corner," I whispered as we seated ourselves at a table with an excellent view of the roiling waves crashing against the pebbled beach below.

Aunt Butty squinted. "Isn't that the woman from the train?"

"Yes. She's an actress. Molly Malloy. Rather well known in the West End. I saw her in a play once. Not bad. A little racy."

"I wonder if she's doing a play here?" my aunt mused.

"I've no idea. I'm more curious about the man with her. Do you know him?" Aunt Butty knew nearly everyone who was anyone.

She gave him a good hard stare. I shifted uncomfortably, but fortunately he seemed too wrapped up in Molly to notice.

"I daresay that's John Goode."

"And who, pray tell, is John Goode?" I asked as the waiter brought us a menu.

Aunt Butty waved him off. "Just bring us an enormous pot of tea and enough cakes to choke a horse."

He blinked but scuttled off to do as he was told. That's the thing about such an upscale hotel. One simply orders what one wants, and it's delivered regardless of how ridiculous. Fortunately, cakes and tea aren't a terribly ridiculous request.

Aunt Butty leaned closer, her amber beads clinking against the edge of the table. "John Goode is a war hero. They claim he saved his entire platoon or some such."

"Interesting. What does he do now?"

"Well, he works in government, as I told you."

I sighed. "Why are there so many people working in government with no particular explanation as to what exactly they do?"

"Oh, I don't believe it's anything mysterious," Aunt Butty assured me. "Not like Varant or Mr. Pennyfather. I'm quite convinced both of those gentlemen are spies. I think Mr. Goode is essentially a pencil pusher, though a powerful one if you're in construction."

"Why's that?"

"He's the one that awards government contracts for public works and such. Or so I hear."

"This is an awfully expensive hotel for a public servant," I said. "Even one in such a position."

"You are so suspicious, Ophelia. Perhaps she's paying for it. As you are always telling me, this is the modern era. Oh, look. Here come our treats!"

Sure enough, the waiter arrived with our tea. Behind him came a second waiter with a large platter of small cakes which he placed gently in the center of the table. There was a simple white sponge filled with apricot preserves covered in sweet, sticky yellow icing, the typical tea cake, toasted and buttered, classic lemon drizzle slices, lovely thick slices of fragrant coffee and walnut cake, and little squares of rich, moist chocolate cake. It really was enough cake to choke a horse.

While Aunt Butty poured tea, I selected a piece of cake. I decided on chocolate, because in my opinion chocolate is life.

I bit into it and it was everything I hoped it would be—moist, rich, melt-in-the mouth scrumptiousness.

Sweet—but not sickeningly so—and ever so chocolatey. I may or may not have let out a little moan.

"I think I'll have some of that, too," Aunty Butty said, helping herself to two pieces of chocolate cake. "Now where were we?"

"A public servant at an expensive hotel. Do you think they're lovers?"

She snorted as she dug into her cake. "What else? Although he's not married, as far as I know, so it isn't like he's cheating on anyone. And she isn't married either. I don't know why he'd feel the need to sneak about."

"I doubt an actress would be considered appropriate wife material for a public servant," I mused. "Especially not one like Molly Malloy. Perhaps that's why."

"What's wrong with her?" Aunt Butty took a large bite of cake. Her moan was loud enough to startle the waiter.

"Rumor has it she's something of a Marxist," I said. "Although I've no idea if that's true or not. Still, it's enough to make her entirely unsuitable as far as his employment is concerned."

"No wonder they don't want to be seen together in London." Aunt Butty polished off her second piece of chocolate cake and selected a slice of lemon drizzle. "In Brighton, simply no one cares."

She wasn't wrong about that. Brighton was far more liberal than London insofar as the acceptance of alternate ways of living and thinking. It wasn't uncommon for those of artistic persuasion to flee the city and take up residence in the seaside resort, away from accusatory glances and gossiping mouths.

"Be that as it may, that is not why we are here," she continued. "We are here about the mystery which our Mr. Singh has brought us."

"Yes. The death, possibly by murder, of Emily Pearson," I agreed, picking up a teacake. As I munched on it, I mulled over our next steps. "We need to find someone with knowledge of those who worked at the hospital back then. Perhaps a nurse or doctor now retired and still living here in Brighton. There surely must be plenty who were either from here originally or stayed here. Emily's friend Dorothy would be ideal if she's still at the address on the envelope."

"I agree that should be our first call, but you know who else we should speak to?" Aunt Butty said, taking a sip of tea. "The groundskeeper. He would know plenty about comings and goings. Bct he could point us in the right direction."

"Wonderful idea. Even though the Pavilion is closed currently, the groundskeeper is probably still working. We can go have a word with him today. After we visit Dorothy."

Aunt Butty glanced outside at the rain slashing against the window. The waves were a grim, gray froth and the sky overhead was twilight dark.

"In this weather? I think not. We'll catch our deaths. I suggest we curl up by the fire with hot toddies and good books and enjoy an afternoon of relaxation. We can question the groundskeeper tomorrow."

"I did not come prepared for an overnight stay," I protested.

"Ophelia, one should always be prepared for any occasion." She tsked. "There are plenty of shops around. You can simply buy something to wear for tomorrow."

"Which would entail leaving the hotel. If we're going to leave the hotel, we might as well start our investigation today."

She sighed heavily. "Very well. If you insist." She popped a chunk of white sponge in her mouth.

"I do," I muttered. "I really do."

"It's nearly luncheon. We can go after that."

"Luncheon?" I stared at her aghast. "We just ate our weight in cake. How can you possibly still be hungry?"

"I'm not," she admitted. "But I hate to miss the most important meal of the day."

"I thought that was breakfast."

"Any meal of the day I'm currently eating is the most important," she said. She eyed the half dozen cakes still sitting on the tray. "I don't suppose they'll let us take these with us. We might get hungry on the journey."

I may have groaned aloud.

It was decided that Mr. Singh and I would visit Dorothy Evans on our own. Although it had been a long time ago, she at least knew who Mr. Singh was and so might consider him a friendly face. One stranger—me—was quite enough. We didn't want to scare her off by descending upon her en masse.

The address was an Edwardian rowhouse a mere few blocks from the Royal Pavilion. Convenient for a person stationed there, I'd imagine.

Up and down the street, standing at attention like elegant soldiers, each plaster façade had been painted a unique color so that they looked like a veritable ice cream rainbow: mint, baby blue, pink, lavender. The window and door trims had been kept white, but the doors were painted to match the walls. The frontages butted right up to the pavement with no front garden at all. One simply walked in from the street.

I rapped the tarnished brass doorknocker—shaped like the anchor of a ship—while Mr. Singh stood back, hands neatly crossed behind him, a very proper butler. It had been agreed that, being a woman and English, I would be the more likely of us to get information from whomever opened the door. Which was the whole reason he'd involved me in the first place. I was under no illusion that I'd make a better detective than he would, should he put his mind to it.

At last the door was opened, and a young woman with pale, freckled skin and pale, carroty hair stood blinking at us. She'd a feather duster in one hand and was clutching a bucket with the other, and her slight frame was swathed in a massive apron underneath which she wore a simple cotton day dress that looked a bit on the worn side.

"Hello," I said cheerfully. "Is Miss Evans at home?"

The girl frowned and scratched the back of her right calf with her left foot. "Don't know no Miss Evans."

"Well, then, how about the lady of the house?"

She squinted up at the ceiling above her as if to glean inspiration. Apparently, she must have received it for she returned her unblinking gaze to mine. "Can I say who is calling?"

I opened my mouth to answer but was cut short when a plump woman bustled up. "Amy, stop gawping at the visitors and get back to your chores."

Amy stared at her a moment, then said slowly, "Yes, mum," before slinking off up a set of stairs.

When she was gone, her mum turned back to us. "So sorry about that. My daughter isn't exactly the brightest, I'm afraid. I'm Mrs. Mullins."

"Ophelia, Lady Rample," I said. "I'm here to visit my dear friend, Dorothy Evans."

Mrs. Mullins's eyes widened at my title, and she quickly whipped off her stained apron, revealing a faded blue cotton dress which she smoothed over and over with nervous hands. "Oh, my. We rarely get such auspicious visitors. I'd invite you in but… well, the parlor rug is rolled up. Spring cleaning you see…"

"Not to worry. I'm just here to say hello to Miss Evans and invite her to tea." As if my stomach could fit another thing after all that cake.

"Well, that's a problem, you see." Mrs. Mullins looked distressed. "Miss Evans did used to rent a room from me, but she no longer lives here."

"Oh?" I made a dramatic effort, pulling the letter from my beaded handbag. "She wrote me, you see. From this address. Admittedly, the letter is a bit old. It got lost in the post."

"I'll say. Miss Evans moved out sixteen years ago, right after the war."

"How disappointing," I wailed. "I was so looking forward to seeing her again. I don't suppose you know where she's got to?"

"No, I don't, I'm afraid. You see, she got married," Mrs. Mullins said.

"Why, that's wonderful. I suppose it was to Johnny." I pulled a name from thin air. "She was mad for him, you see."

"I can't speak as to that," Mrs. Mullins admitted. "I don't recall she ever told me the gentleman's name, but I know they moved to London right after."

"I don't suppose you know what part of London?" I asked.

"Indeed not." Mrs. Mullins looked terribly distressed. "I'm so sorry. I wish I could have been of more help."

"Not to worry," I reassured her. "I'm certain she'll write another letter."

"Oh, yes. She was always writing letters, that one."

As Mr. Singh and I walked away from Mrs. Mullins's boarding house, I kicked rather viciously at a stray rock. It skittered across the pavement and tumbled into the street. "Well, that's a dead end. We'll never find her in London without even a last name to go on."

"Unfortunately, you are correct."

I couldn't tell from his expression—or lack thereof—if he was angry, disappointed, or completely unmoved by our dead end. "I'm afraid we've no alternative but to try Aunt Butty's idea and accost complete strangers."

I swear I saw his lips twitch.

It was Simon who joined us on our sojourn to the Pavilion, Mr. Singh having gone off on some errand or other. He'd been very cagey about it. I was surprised he didn't want to join us, but Aunt Butty assured me Mr. Singh knew what he was doing. Of that I had no doubt.

"He's got other fish to fry, Lady Ophelia," Simon assured me as he wove in and out of traffic, headed up the steeply inclined street. At least it had stopped raining.

"Does he now," I muttered. Well, that wasn't much of a surprise. Mr. Singh... such a mystery.

Simon pulled into the car park, shut off the engine, and hopped out to assist us. "Should I wait with the car, Lady Butty? Or would you like me to accompany you?" He threw back his shoulders and puffed up his chest, as if to make himself look more intimidating.

It didn't work. Simon was reed thin and looked all of about fifteen, even though he was closer to my own thirty-something. Although, if you looked closely, you could see someone far older in his eyes. It came with having served in the Great War, I suppose. I sometimes wondered if you could see the same thing in my own eyes. I may have been a nurse and far removed from the front, but I'd still seen more things than I wanted to recall.

"You stay here, Simon," Aunt Butty said, adjusting her massive red had covered in white ostrich feathers. "I think Ophelia and I can manage one gardener on our own." And she took off at a brisk march around the Pavilion.

The place was a marvel of creamy stone and onion-shaped turrets. Like something out of *1001 Arabian Nights*. At any moment, Scheherazade was going to come dancing out of the castle with her colorful veils floating behind her.

Instead, as we rounded the building, we came upon a figure in a rain slicker, hunched over an azalea. Based on the fact he was snipping away at the bush with a pair of shears, and there was a wheelbarrow filled with clippings behind him, I was betting this was the groundskeeper.

Aunt Butty cleared her throat as we drew near. "Excuse me. Sir? Pardon me! May we have a word?"

The groundskeeper straightened slowly and turned around. We saw our mistake immediately.

"Er, sorry, madam," Aunt Butty muttered. "Stupid assumption."

The woman—for it was very definitely a woman—was quite tall, nearing six feet, with a figure of Amazonian proportions. Beneath her rain hat hung two iron gray braids neatly tied off with garden twine. Her face was brown as shoe leather and heavily lined as though she spent a great deal of time out of doors. Which, I suppose she did, being a groundskeeper.

"Ain't the first time I been mistook. Been happening my whole life." She eyed us up and down, shears still firmly grasped in both hands. "Pavilion's closed today."

"Yes, we know," Aunt Butty assured her. "We didn't come for the Pavilion. We came for you."

One salt and pepper eyebrow rose. "Me? That's a new 'un." She carefully laid the shears in the wheelbarrow. "What can I do for two fine ladies such as yourselves."

Was it just me, or was her tone ever so slightly mocking? It was hard to tell. "I am Ophelia, Lady Rample and this is my aunt, Lady Lucas."

"Jane Moore." Not a woman to mince words, apparently.

"We are looking for someone who worked here during the Great War while the palace was a hospital," I said. "Were you here then?"

Jane snorted. "Hardly. I'd other things to do.
Husband, James, was groundskeeper back then. Too old to
join the war, so he stayed on here. Not just the grounds,
but inside, too."

"Could we speak to him then?" Aunt Butty asked.
"It's very important."

"Wouldn't do you any good."

"Well, surely if we explained, he would understand
the situation," my aunt pressed.

"Doubt it. 'Less you're a witch."

Aunt Butty blinked.

"Excuse me?" My tone was just this side of a snarl.

"He's dead," Jane said. "Buried down in the church
yard like any good Christian man. Whatever you needed
from him, well, good luck with it unless you can raise the
dead."

Aunt Butty swore in a not at all ladylike fashion.

Jane didn't look at all shocked. Instead she picked
up her shears and went back to shaping the azalea.

"Isn't there anyone around who was here back
then?" I asked. "Anyone we could talk to?"

She paused, lifting her eyes to the gloomy sky as if in thought. "There might be one or two around from back then."

"Here? In Brighton?" I asked.

"Last I heard. You could talk to Johnny Brice. Hardly more'n a kid back then and a bum leg to boot, but he was here and could maybe point you in the right direction. Then there was Mildred Pierce. Now she didn't work at the hospital or anything, but there ain't a thing goes on in this town she don't know about."

She gave us brief directions, which I hoped Simon could follow, and then turned her back on us as if to say that's the end of that. And I suppose it was.

We trooped back to the car where Simon quickly stubbed out a ciggie before jumping to help us into the vehicle. "Hope all went well, miladies."

"In a manner of speaking," I said. "We have a couple more stops, if you don't mind."

"No worries, Lady O. Let me fire up Ole Bessy and we'll be on our way. Where to?"

"Old Bessie?" I mouthed to my aunt who shrugged.

"If it makes him happy," she whispered loud enough he probably heard her. In an even louder voice, she gave him directions. "And step on it, lad. The game's afoot."

Clearly Aunt Butty had been reading too much detective fiction again.

Chapter 4

Our first stop was at the tenant house where Johnny Brice lived. His landlady answered the door in a swirl of fried-onion-scented steam. She wore a severe black gown and bore an even more severe expression. Her black hair was highlighted with bits of silver like tinsel and done up in a tight bun. She was the exact opposite of Mrs. Mullins other than her generous proportions. "Whatchu want?" she asked in a heavy Italian accent, thick eyebrows lowering ominously.

"Hello, my name is Lady Lucas," Aunt Butty said in her poshest accent. "This is my niece, Lady Rample. And you are?"

"Signora Linnetti." She propped her hands on her wide hips. "Why you wanna know?"

"We would like to speak to Johnny Brice, *per favore*, Signora. It is *most* important," Aunt Butty said.

"Why you want him?"

"He's an old family friend," I lied through my teeth.

"Huh." I don't think she bought it. "He not here. He working."

"Oh?" I widened my eyes. "Is he still working up at the Pavilion?"

"No. He working down at tobacco shop. You go there." And she slammed the door in our faces.

"Well!" Aunt Butty huffed.

"Wouldn't want to tangle with her in a dark alley," I muttered.

"Do you know of a nearby tobacconist's, Simon?" Aunt Butty asked as we climbed back in the car.

"One just down the street, milady," Simon said cheerfully. "You want I should stop there?"

"Yes, please."

We'd hardly caught our breath before he was pulling up in front of the tobacconists. It was a narrow building crammed in between a greengrocer and a second-hand shop. A faded sign above the door read "Duber and Sons, Tobacconist." The dusty window was plastered with flyers and advertisements for every sort of tobacco, pipe accessory, and cigarette paper one could imagine.

"You sure you want to go in there?" Simon asked. "Looks a mite dodgy to me."

"Unfortunately, Simon, we must go where the clues take us," I said. "And in this instance, they're taking us here."

He sighed heavily and climbed out of the car and opened the door for us. "Well, then, I'll be going with you."

"Unnecessary," Aunt Butty insisted. "We'll be fine on our own."

"No doubt, milady, but Mr. Singh. He'd have my head."

There was no arguing with that, so we didn't grumble as Simon held the door to the tobacconists for us.

As we stepped inside, we were hit with a wall of sweet tobacco and heavy musk. The room was dim and oppressive, a high counter ringing off most of the room with all the wares safely behind it. Perched on a stool next to the register was a young man of perhaps twenty-six or seven.

He'd flaxen hair, already thinning on top, and a sallow complexion—no doubt from too much time spent indoors. His frame was almost fragile, shoulders slightly hunched as he studied a magazine.

"Johnny Brice?" Aunt Butty asked without further ado.

He glanced up and upon seeing two ladies and their uniformed chauffeur in his shop, struggled off the stool. "Yes, madam. May I help you?" He gave her a boyish smile as he limped closer to the counter.

"We were just up at the palace and spoke to the groundskeeper there. Mrs. Moore. She thought perhaps you could help us," Aunt Butty said.

A frown line creased his otherwise smooth brow. "Well, unless you want tobacco, I don't know how I can help you. If it's anything to do with the shop, you gotta talk to Mr. Duber. He's the owner."

"And is he here today?" I asked, not wanting to be interrupted by Johnny's boss.

"No madam. He's not."

"It's 'my lady,'" Simon muttered.

Johnny blushed right to the roots of his hair. "Er, sorry. My lady."

I waved off his apologies. "What about 'and sons?'"

"Isn't any. See, Mr. Duber himself was the 'and sons.' Or one of them anyway. His brother was killed in the Great War, and he inherited the shop. Kept the name because he thinks it sounds important. Had to hire the likes of me to help out, though." He shook his head. "So none around who can help I'm afraid."

"That's perfectly all right," Aunt Butty said soothingly. "It's you we came to see. We want to know about your time at the palace during the Great War. When it was a hospital."

His eyes widened a fraction. "Really? Why? That was ever so long ago."

"You see," I told him, "we are trying to find an old friend. We thought maybe you'd remember her."

"Her?" He blushed a little. "Like a nurse you mean?"

"How'd you know we were talkin' about a nurse?" Simon asked suspiciously.

Johnny's flush deepened. "They were pretty much the only women that worked up there. So I-I just assumed."

"You're spot on, Johnny," I said soothingly, shooting Simon a glare for upsetting the young man. "We're looking for a nurse named Emily Pearson."

He went a little pale. "Oh, I'm sorry, miss—"

Simon cleared his throat.

"I mean, my lady." Johnny sank down on his stool as if his legs could no longer hold him. "Didn't you hear?"

"Hear what?" I asked, playing dumb. Aunt Butty put on a matching expression of innocence.

"Well, miss—my lady—Nurse Emily, she was real sweet, see. Nice to everybody, even folks like me that emptied slop pails and scrubbed surgery floors and the like. Always kind to the patients even though some folks didn't like 'em because they were from India and all. But the reason I remember so clear is one night, she vanished."

"Vanished?" Aunt Butty gasped as if she'd never heard of such a thing. She deserved an award for playacting.

"Yes, my lady. Just up and vanished in the middle of the night. Whole hospital was abuzz. She was never a minute late and one day she doesn't show? Her and her things gone from her flat? I didn't buy it, but the police said there was nothin' they could do and we all just went on about our business."

"Ghastly," Aunt Butty said, clutching her throat. I thought she was laying it on a bit thick.

"And then it wasn't but two days later, they found her drowned in the pond up there next to the Royal Pavilion. Like something right out of a play by that Shakespeare fellow."

He meant Ophelia, of course, who'd drown herself after being rejected by Hamlet. Yes, I bore her name. However, I'd never had even the slightest inclination toward offing myself over a man. "So she killed herself then?"

He shrugged. "Maybe yes. Maybe no. Police said it was suicide. Some said it was an accident."

"What do you say?" Simon asked.

He shrugged again. "Not my place. But I will say this. That Nurse Emily, I don't reckon she was the sort to go and off herself. Not like that. She was afraid of water, see. I heard her brother drowned when he was a baby. Something like that. So I don't see how it was an accident, either. She kept well away from that pond. Everyone knew about it."

Everyone knew about Emily's fear of water. How very interesting.

"Do you know where Nurse Emily came from?" Aunt Butty asked. "Where her people are?"

"Might do," he admitted.

"Johnny." I pulled a pad of paper and a pencil from my handbag. "Write it down, please. Everything you know."

As he did, I thought I should also ask about Dorothy Evans.

"Sorry, miss. My lady. Don't rightly remember her. Will this be alright?" He handed me a piece of paper with an address awkwardly scrawled on it.

"That'll do just fine."

By the time we exited Duber and Sons Tobacconist, it was chucking down rain again. Deep puddles had formed across the pavement and cars sent up sheets of water as they zipped by. We decided to forgo speaking to Mildred Pierce and instead return to the hotel and its warm fires and hot toddies.

While Aunt Butty went straight to her room, I stopped in the lobby to use the telephone. John Goode, the man I'd seen with Molly Malloy was sitting on a bench across from the booth reading a newspaper. He gave me a funny look as I walked past, but I figured it was due to my bedraggled state and put it from my mind.

Leaving the door to the booth open a crack as I dislike small spaces, I placed a call to Maddie with instructions to get herself down to Brighton with my overnight case. I'd no doubt we were in for a few more days stay.

"Is Hale in?" I asked her once she'd taken down my list of items to bring.

"No milady. He left for practice an hour ago, but I'll be sure and send him a note."

"Thank you, Maddie." I didn't let on my disappointment. I'd just have to ring him later.

Next, I rang Louise Pennyfather. Aunt Butty had said she knew a lot of people in Brighton. Perhaps she knew something about Emily Pearson's death. At the very least, she'd have been sure to have heard gossip about it.

Louise herself picked up. I recognized her stentorian tones immediately.

"Louise, it's Ophelia," I said without preamble. Louise was not the sort of person who enjoyed small talk.

"Oh, Ophelia, how are you? I've been meaning to ring. Your aunt and I have been talking about putting on a seance. What do you think?"

"Sounds marvelous. Listen, Aunt Butty says you're quite familiar with Brighton society."

"Such as it is," Louise confirmed.

"I'm trying to find out more about the death of a young woman who worked as a nurse at the Indian Hospital during the war." I quickly told her what I knew about Emily.

"Beastly business," Louise said when I'd finished catching her up. "Poor young thing. Quite pretty she was, too. From a decent, middle class family. Nothing special, mind, but solid country folk. The backbone of England."

"But do you know anything about what happened?"

"Only what one reads in the papers. However, I do have a friend who may be able to help."

"Oh, that would be marvelous, Louise. Thank you."

"His name is Dominic Parlance, and he's one of those theater people. You know the type." The sound of flipping pages rattled through the line.

"Ah, sure. Yes." I had no idea what she meant.

"Here's his number. Are you ready?" She rattled off a telephone number which I quickly jotted down in my little notebook. "He knows everyone who is anyone and anything there is to know about everything. If he can't help you, I doubt anyone can."

"Thank you, darling." But she'd already hung up.

I let myself out of the booth, shutting it neatly behind me before striding to the front desk to check for messages. There were none, so I made my way to the lift, meaning to freshen up as best I could before joining Aunt Butty for supper.

The lift slid open and I was about to step into the car when something pressed into the small of my back. It felt rather like the barrel of a gun!

"Don't make a sound," a gravelly voice said in my ear. "Come with me, or I'll shoot you dead."

Shéa MacLeod

Chapter 5

Deciding cooperation was the better part of virtue, I obliged the gentleman currently pressing a gun into the small of my back as he frog-marched me across the lobby toward the street. The desk clerk looked up, startled, as we strode past.

"My lady, is everything all right?"

"Peachy!" I called back. "Tell my aunt I'm not the least bit hungry and am going for a stroll along the promenade."

There. That ought to do it. For one, Aunt Butty has never known me to not be hungry. For another, the day I went voluntarily for exercise was the day Hell froze over.

She'd know something was wrong immediately. Though what she'd do about it was anyone's guess. Knowing Aunt Butty, it could be anything from calling the police—unlikely—to hiring circus clowns—more likely.

My escort and I pushed through the front door, dodged raindrops down the steps, and hurried into a waiting car. Long and black with its motor running. That was all I could tell. The driver wore a cheap suit with a fedora pulled low—although it did not cover the narrow scar along his cheek—and an unlit cigarette dangling from his mouth. My companion was a near carbon copy, minus the cigarette and scar and plus a revolver. Marvelous. I did so enjoy being kidnapped. It was getting to be a regular habit with me.

The car roared off down the street, nearly bowling over a priest who was strolling along minding his own business. The tires screeched as we turned a corner, headed up the hill, and through neighborhoods of narrow Victorian brick townhouses which eventually gave way to leafier streets lined with newer single-family homes.

Finally, as the sun such as it was slid low upon the horizon, we emerged into the countryside. Green pastures stretched out on either side of the road, dotted with fleecy white sheep and brown, speckled cows. The traffic thinned out to nothing and the houses were few and far between. Help of any kind grew increasingly unlikely. I might have gripped the door handle a little tighter than necessary.

By the time we pulled onto a rutted drive, I was feeling some trepidation. This was a little more than the usual kidnap and threaten situation. We were a long way from anything vaguely resembling civilization and fear crept like icy fingers up my spine. It was all I could do to force it back and put on a brave face.

The car bounced and jarred its way up the drive, finally emerging onto a wide, graveled parking area over which loomed a gothic manor that was enough to strike fear into the hearts of the most steadfast. I was absolutely certain Count Dracula was in residence.

The man with the gun clambered out and gave a little wave of the weapon. Not being entirely stupid, I got out, too. Together, we climbed the shallow steps to the door. My captor rapped once with a large gargoyle doorknocker, and the door swung open to reveal the sour visage of a middle-aged woman to whom life had no doubt handed a great deal of lemons. I could have told her said lemons made for excellent lemon drops, but it seemed unwise to mention it.

"Is he in?" my captor asked in his gravelly voice.

"He'll be down shortly. You can wait in the library." She turned and strode away, sensible heels clacking on the parquet floor.

We stepped over the threshold and followed. The driver was apparently staying with the car.

The library was as expected. Rows upon rows of dark shelving lined the walls, each holding neat rows of leather-bound books, all precisely the same size and color. It was not a reader's library like my own at home—stuffed to the gills with works of fiction covered in bright colors—but the sort of place someone had paid a lot of money to create so they would come across as intelligent and well read.

A fire burned low in the grate, adding some measure of warmth to the seating area which consisted of a lovely-but-inexpensive Chinese rug, two brown leather club chairs, and a brown velvet settee. It would have been a perfect place for relaxing except for the fact I was not exactly there by choice.

"Stay here," Gravel Voice grunted before stepping out of the room and closing the door behind him. There was a distinctive click. Wonderful. I was locked in.

Since I wasn't getting out that way, I tried the French doors which faced out to the garden. They were bolted. The sort which require keys to get out, and while I may technically know how to pick locks, it takes a great deal of time and concentration. Well, there was nothing for it. I'd have to bide my time and see what arose.

In the meantime, I wasn't about to sit idly by and await my fate. The minute I got the chance, I was going to head for the hills. Unfortunately, I'd little idea where I was or how to get back to Brighton save on the main road, which seemed a poor choice as I doubted my captors would let me go willingly.

A large cabinet was set against one wall. I opened it to reveal rows of liquor bottles including one exceptionally expensive bottle of scotch. I figured since the owner of the bottle had me kidnapped, he owed me. Beside which, I could stand to steady my nerves. Pulling out the stopper, I took a slug. Very nice. Returning the bottle after a second swallow, I took stock of the rest of the room.

There was a large rosewood desk positioned between the two windows, facing the door. No telephone, alas, though there was a writing tray next to on which was a neat stack of unopened envelopes. I picked up the top one. It was addressed to Mr. R. Haigh. A quick peek through the rest of the stack revealed more envelopes addressed to the same person and postmarked from various places around the globe. No doubt today's post.

So whoever this Mr. R. Haigh was, he was responsible for my kidnapping. What I wanted to know was, why? As far as I remembered, I'd never met anyone called Haigh. And I'd certainly never been to this house or even spent much time in this part of the country. Could it possibly have something to do with our investigation? But if so, how? No one but Aunt Butty, myself, Mr. Singh, and our other compatriots knew about it. Perhaps one of the people we'd questioned was in on it! Although that didn't seem likely.

I carefully replaced the envelopes and turned my attention to the desk drawers, hoping for weapon of some kind—a letter opener, perhaps—a map, or some other indication of how close the nearest village was. From there

I could ring the hotel and get Simon to collect me. If I could get out of here.

Oddly, there was no weapon to be had. Clearly someone had gone through the room and removed all the sharp objects. What I found in the very bottom drawer was a copy of the *ABC Railway Guide*. Which wouldn't have done me any good except that some helpful person had dogeared one of the pages and circled one of the stations in red: Falmer. It must be the closest station. I vaguely remembered seeing it on the way in. Question was, how far away was I from Falmer?

Fortunately, there was a foldout map. Using a bit of logic and a bit of guesswork, I figured out which way the car had gone out of Brighton and followed it along more or less in the direction of Falmer. However, I was much further out in the countryside than Falmer was. From my best guess, I was at least four or five miles away. Which, while doable, was a bit of a walk. Likely I'd be caught if they figured out what I was doing. I would have to put more consideration into my escape.

Without further thought, I ripped the map out of the guide, folded it, and stuffed it into my brassiere. If they searched my handbag, I did not want them finding it. Then

I shoved the guide back in the drawer, shut it softly, and dashed over to perch casually on the settee.

Just in time. The lock rattled and the door was thrust open dramatically. A small man stood in the doorway posed in a Napoleonic fashion with one hand tucked beneath the breast of his jacket. Behind him was the man who'd held me at gunpoint, Gravel Voice.

Napoleon reminded me suddenly of an acquaintance of mine, Sir Eustace. Sir Eustace and his wife, Lady Mary, had once upon a time invited me to a party at their London home. It was shortly after I'd come out of mourning, and I'd have rather been anywhere but listening to Sir Eustace drone on about his—no doubt falsified— African adventures.

Like Sir Eustace, this man had enormous muttonchop sideburns. Terribly unfashionable. He also had a waxed moustache, a pot belly, and a ruddy complexion. To top it all off, he wore thick-lensed spectacles and a top hat indoors. Other than being a very solid five-foot- nine— Sir Eustace was hardly more than five-one—the two could have been twins. There was something dashed odd about the whole thing… as if Mr. Napoleon wasn't entirely real.

Before he could speak, I stood up and demanded in an imperious voice, "What is the meaning of this! I demand you release me at once." Aunt Butty would have been so proud.

"Now, now," Sir Eustace's twin murmured in what he no doubt thought as a soothing tone, although his voice was a bit high-pitched and rather grating. "Please do not upset yourself, dear lady. We simply have a bit of business to discuss."

I eyeballed him. "I don't know why we would. I've never met you before in my life."

That seemed to amuse him. "No? Ah, well, allow me to introduce myself. I am Mr. Haigh."

"That means nothing to me." I didn't mention I already knew his name. I didn't want him realizing I'd been going through his desk and put two-and-two together. It would spoil my escape plans for sure.

"No surprise there." He sat down, took out a cigar, and lit it without so much as asking. Clearly, he was no gentleman. "You see, Mrs. Rample... may I call you Mrs. Rample?"

I sniffed. "It's *Lady* Rample."

I swear he smirked, but it was hard to tell under the mustache. "Very good, my *lady*. You and I have some business to discuss. Please sit."

I did so reluctantly. "I don't know what possible business we could have."

"I'm speaking about your little... investigation."

I could only assume he meant my looking into the death of Emily Pearson. "What has that got to do with you?"

"That, my lady, is neither here nor there. But I would like you to leave off."

I snorted. "Leave off? I don't think so."

A muscled flexed in his jaw. "It would be in your best interests to cooperate, my lady. Otherwise..."

"Otherwise?" I arched a brow, hoping I looked elegant and cool.

"Otherwise it could be very... uncomfortable for you."

It was my turn to flex a muscle. "I don't like being threatened, Mr. Haigh."

He laughed and flicked cigar ash on the carpet. "No one does." His expression turned threatening. "However, I suggest you comply. Otherwise that aunt of yours could have a very bad accident. The elderly are prone to such, or so I hear."

"How dare you threaten my aunt!" I hissed. Aunt Butty would no doubt be more outraged that he'd called her elderly than that he'd threatened her person.

Haigh leaned forward, expression intent. "I want you to understand I'm quite serious. I suggest you beat it back to London. Forget the whole thing." The "or else" was very clear in his tone. "In the meantime, I think you need some time to think it over." He beckoned to Gravel Voice. "Show Lady Rample to a room."

I didn't like the sound of that, but once again, Gravel Voice was armed and clearly not afraid to use his weapon. He held the little snub-nosed revolver on me all the way up the stairs which were lined with portraits of Haight's frowning ancestors where he let me into a very elaborate guest suite before once again locking me in. He never once asked to search either my handbag or my person.

"Well, I never." I banged on the door more for show than anything. "Let me out, or you'll regret it!"

Naturally, I was completely ignored. Very well. I would do what I must.

Unlike the ground floor, the windows of the guest room were unlocked. No doubt they figured that a woman of my age and position wouldn't go jumping out of first floor windows. They didn't know me very well.

I cautiously checked to make sure there was no one in sight before sliding up to the window. I poked my head out and had a good look around. Below me was a bed of crocuses. Not nearly soft enough to break my fall from two stories up. However, halfway along the wall was a trellis which would allow me to climb down quite easily. If only I could get to it.

Fortunately, there was a ledge that ran along under the windows. Perfect. I leaned back in and kicked off my heels, tucking them into the large pockets of my overcoat. I unclipped my stockings, rolled them down my legs, and tucked them into my handbag which I hitched up onto my shoulder. Then I hiked up the skirt of my dress to mid-thigh and sat on the windowsill and cautiously swung one leg over the edge.

It took a heart-stopping moment of feeling around the freezing stone with my bare foot. At last, I found the ledge and eased myself out the window, quickly attaining the ledge with my other foot.

My feet were quickly numbed with cold, which didn't bode well for nimbleness as I edged along the ledge, using the window frames as hand grips. It took only a matter of a minute to ease over to the next window. I peered inside to make sure there was no one there to see me.

It was a guest room, much like the one I'd been put into, only done up in gold tones instead of green. It was also empty. I quickly moved past it.

The trellis was beneath the third window. Again, I peered inside to find yet another guest room. Red this time. It looked not unlike what I imagined a bordello would look like. Mr. Haigh definitely had questionable taste.

Now came the difficult part. I'd have to get down the trellis, hopefully without it breaking on me and without anyone spotting me. Then I'd have to make a run for it. Only I'd yet to determine in which direction lay Falmer.

The wooden trellis creaked ominously underneath my foot. "Oh, dear."

No choice but to go for broke. I put my full weight on it. It waggled wildly beneath me. I wrapped my hands around it in a death grip, closed my eyes, and sucked in a deep breath. Then I opened them and slowly, slowly began climbing down.

I was perhaps halfway when there was a horrendous crack. The wood beneath my feet gave way, and I plummeted to the ground!

Chapter 6

They say that right before you die, your life flashes before your eyes. I can tell you for a fact that no such thing happens. It's rather more of a string of expletives unrepeatable in public. In my particular case, that string was cut short when I landed with a *whomp* in an azalea bush.

It was rather poky and dashed uncomfortable, but at least I was alive, and I hadn't broken anything. I blinked up at the rapidly darkening sky as my brain tried to reconnect with my body. I was just heaving myself out of the bush when I heard a shout.

Dash it all, my escape had been discovered!

I unsnarled myself, relocated my handbag, and started off across the lawn, unsure where I was headed. The grass was prickly, and mud oozed between my bare toes. I could barely feel it as they were already numb from cold. Another shout, and I turned to see the gunman rounding the side of the house, followed by the driver.

Letting out a string of unladylike words, I hiked up my skirt and dashed across the lawn toward the front of the house. As I rounded the corner, I saw that both cars were unattended. I was betting the little sporty number belonged to the man who'd had me kidnapped. As far as I was concerned, he owed me.

I winced as my bare feet hit gravel, but I didn't slow down. Reaching the car, I yanked open the door, tossed in my handbag and jumped in, accidentally sitting on one of my shoes, still in the pocket of my coat. With a curse, I yanked the shoes out of my pockets and settled back into the driver's seat. I jabbed the starter button and the motor roared to life.

Something pinged off the gravel. That jackanapes was shooting at me!

I gunned the engine, released the handbrake, and roared off down the drive. A quick glance in the mirror showed the gunman and the driver hopping in the black motorcar and driving after me, while Haigh stood in the doorway. I couldn't see the expression on his face, but I was betting he was none too happy.

I didn't have time to get my shoes on, so I focused on driving, pushing the sporty vehicle as fast as it would go over the potholed drive. Ahead, the gates stood open— permanently so, based on the ivy wound around them. I zoomed between them and out onto the road.

Behind me, a horn blared, and I winced as I realized I'd cut off a lorry piled high with barrels. It swerved, trying to right itself. Meanwhile, the black car appeared at the end of the drive. I pressed the accelerator, lurching forward.

Ahead was a slow-moving tractor—no doubt headed home for his supper—and, coming from the opposite direction, the local bus. Nothing for it. I sped up, swerved into oncoming traffic, and darted back into my lane with but a hairsbreadth to spare between myself and the bus. More blaring horns. I was getting used to that.

I barely had time to register a sign along the side of the road with an arrow, the number 2, and the name Falmer. I breathed out a shaky sigh. I was on the right track. Two miles to the train station.

Glancing in the rearview mirror again, I could see the black car had gone around the lorry and tractor and was now behind me, though some ways back, its headlights glaring in the ever-increasing darkness. I pressed harder on the accelerator. Aunt Butty would have my head if she saw me driving like this.

Still the black car crept closer. I couldn't see men inside, but I hoped they didn't start shooting again.

The road branched, and I waited until the last minute to veer left. The black car shot past on the main road, and I chortled to myself. "Falmer, here I come."

I didn't slow down, though, just in case. I zipped past hedgerows and fields and over a narrow little bridge. I may or may not have slightly scraped the paint.

There was a slight rise in the road before it cascaded down into a charming little village nestled among the trees, lights glowing as if in welcome. I blew past the village pub earning myself more than a few stares, rounded the duck pond, and finally emerged onto the road leading to the train station.

I would have liked to hide the car, but there was no time. I could already see train pulling into the station, the word BRIGHTON clear even in the waning light.

Careening into the car park, I killed the engine, rammed my shoes on my feet, grabbed my handbag and jumped out of the car. I dashed to the ticket window of the little Victorian brick station.

"One ticket to Brighton, please."

The ticket seller glanced up and a look of astonishment crossed his wizened face. I must look a fright. No doubt I'd twigs in my hair, and I was certainly covered in mud. But he said nothing, simply took my money and handed me a ticket.

The train blasted a whistle, and I scurried through the turnstile onto the platform. As I took my seat, I breathed a sigh of relief. I'd evaded my captors. But why had they taken me in the first place? I wasn't the only one investigating Emily's murder. Who were they? What were they trying to hide? Was this Haigh person responsible for her death?

The train let out another blast in preparation for leaving the station. Almost home free.

And then, through the turnstile, came Haigh's gunman and driver. Curses! They'd found me.

They headed straight for the train and climbed aboard. I got up with the thought to exit the train, but it lurched forward. Too late. I was stuck.

I had taken a seat in the second car from the back. They'd gotten on at the very end, no doubt so they could carefully check every car. I'd no other choice, I'd have to move forward toward the front car and hope we reached the next stop before they got to me. It was unlikely I'd make it to Brighton without them catching up.

Easing my way between the seats, I carefully let myself into the next car just as the conductor announced the next station, "Moulsecoomb, next stop."

The train slowed, lurching slightly, and I pushed my way forward to the front of the car. I'd get off here and figure it out from there.

"Ophelia?"

I turned and gasped in shock. "Phil, what are you doing here?"

Philoma "Phil" Dearling was my cousin-in-law, Binky's cousin. Or second cousin. Or something. We'd met recently at Harrods and had hit it off immediately.

Phil was charming with dark hair and big, blue eyes, a lithe figure and an impeccable sense of style. She wore a jaunty little red hat that matched her lipstick and her shoes. A matching red overnight case sat at her feet. "I'm just visiting my aunt for the weekend. She lives in Moulsecoomb. One of the modern houses they built after the war."

"Perfect. Can I come with you?"

If she was surprised or offended by my inviting myself along, she didn't show it. "Of course. But what are you doing here? I'm afraid you look rather a fright, darling."

I touched my hair self-consciously. "I wouldn't be surprised. You see, I've been kidnapped."

This time, she did react. Her perfectly penciled brows rose almost to her hairline. "Oh, do tell. But first, we're almost to the station." She collected her handbag and case and stood, ushering me before her to the end of the car.

We hovered near the door as the train pulled slowly into the station. I willed it to hurry up, but there was no hurrying anything when it came to the railroad. At last, it lurched to a stop and we clambered out.

"I can't let them see me," I told Phil.

"No, of course not. Here." She whipped her hat off her head and crammed it on mine. "Give me your coat."

I did as she ordered.

"Put mine on." She shrugged out of it, only she was quite a bit thinner than me.

In the end, I draped it over my shoulders while she tucked mine over her arm. Since mine was cream and streaked with mud, and hers was a lovely pale blue, my pursuers would likely be thrown off looking for the wrong coat.

Chatting gaily as if we'd not a care in the world, we strolled toward the exit. Just as we passed the last car, a window slid down and a man popped his head out. It was the gunman, Gravel Voice. I tried not to flinch and kept my head tilted just slightly so all he'd see was the red hat and the back of Phil's blue coat. Hopefully he wouldn't notice my feet.

The whistle blasted and the engine chugged as the train prepared to leave the station. The man was just about to pull his head in when a gust of wind grabbed Phil's coat and sent it swirling off my shoulders. Without thinking, I reached to grab it, fully exposing my face to Gravel Voice.

He shouted, but it was too late. The train lurched forward and, picking up speed, pulled out of the station.

Phil grabbed my arm. "Let's beat it before those bozos decide to jump the train."

That was all I needed. We picked up the pace, and I didn't breathe easy until we were out of the station and well on our way to Phil's aunt's.

Phil's aunt lived a few streets away from the station in a semi-detached mock Tudor about a decade old. The bottom half was brick, and the top white stucco was decorated with faux wood beams meant to mimic the half-timbering of the real MacKay. There was no garden to speak of in the front, just a narrow concrete strip decorated with a couple of large ceramic pots filled with daffodils and crocuses just beginning to bloom.

The entire neighborhood was very working class, the houses much smaller than I was used to these days. Even my townhouse was larger than this.

"My aunt is from the un-monied side of the family," Phil said almost apologetically as she rapped on the door. "My uncle was a newspaperman before he died."

"I grew up in a vicarage," I told her.

Her eyes widened. "Now that's a story I've got to hear."

But she wouldn't be hearing it any time soon. The door swung open and a slender woman in a neat-but-plain blue cotton percale house dress topped with a knitted cream-colored cardigan stood in the doorway. Her dark hair was threaded with silver and done in careful-but-simple waves. A pair of wire-rimmed glasses was perched on the end of a long, thin nose—similar to Phil's.

"Phil!" She hugged her niece enthusiastically. "And you've brought a friend."

"Ophelia," I said before Phil could introduce us more formally. I was very familiar with the class in which Phil's aunt moved. It was the same in which I'd grown up. Having a titled lady to visit would no doubt send her all aflutter. A woman did not invite people in while wearing a housedress unless they were family or close friends. My appearance would have had her running for her closet and panicking over the quality of her biscuits.

Phil gave me a grateful look. "Yes, and this is my aunt, Deidre Phillips."

"Lovely to meet you, Mrs. Phillips."

"Oh, call me Aunt Dee," she laughed. "Everyone does. Now come along, you two. Tea's on. You can refresh yourself and then tell me about your travels."

After cleaning up as best I could in the loo, I rejoined my hostess in the kitchen. I wasn't expecting much, seeing as how both Phil and her aunt were extremely slim. In my experience, most slim women simply didn't eat, at least not in company and certainly not in the quantity I preferred. However, Aunt Dee proved to be a marvel in the kitchen. Not only did she brew an excellent spot of tea, but she made the most mouthwatering crumpets, moist cakes, and crumbly biscuits. I was tempted to hire her on the spot as my chef.

We chatted of inane things such as the weather and the price of milk—the latter certainly being a weak spot for me. At Phil's urging, I regaled them with a few of the more interesting tales of growing up a vicar's daughter. Like the time I caught Tommy Tompkins stealing from the collection plate. I suppose one could call it my first case if one were so inclined.

Eventually, Aunt Dee went to refill the teapot and I leaned over and whispered to Phil, "I don't suppose your aunt would let me use the telephone?"

"Aunt Dee doesn't have one," she said. "There's one down at the corner shop, though. That's where I ring when I need to get a message to her."

"Oh, right." I had to remember that most people didn't have telephones in their homes. Although I imagined that one day, everyone would. "You don't suppose she'd be offended if I went and made a call do you? Only my aunt has no idea where I am, and I'll need a ride to Brighton."

"Of course not. And you can come back here to wait once you've rung. Hurry along. I think she's bringing out her ginger cake next."

More cake? I was bound to be busting my buttons any moment. I don't know how Phil managed it.

I quickly made my excuses—Aunt Dee was most understanding—and hurried out of the house in the direction I'd been given. I kept a keen eye out for Haigh or his flunkies. I doubted they were anywhere near this neighborhood, but one could never be too careful.

The red phone booth stood out clearly against the white-washed wall of the shop despite the fact it was fully dark now. Fortunately, I always carried a few coins with me for emergencies, and I was quickly put through to the hotel. I thought about asking for Aunt Butty—who was no doubt frantic by now—but found myself instead requesting to speak with Mr. Singh.

There was a long pause, and then in a tone rife with astonishment, "The butler?"

"I will not repeat myself, young man," I snapped.

"Y-yes, Miss."

"That's 'my lady' to you, young jackanapes."

I could almost feel the blood drain from his face even through the line. It wasn't terribly often I played the title card, but sometimes I find it very satisfying.

I was on hold so long I had to add coins to the machine, but at last Mr. Singh came on the line. I immediately breathed easier. "Mr. Singh, I have a bit of a conundrum."

"Then you have come to the right place. How may I assist you, my lady? We have been most worried."

"I'm alright. I've had a bit of an adventure, and I need a ride." I gave him Aunt Dee's address.

"I will be there within the hour." And he rang off after promising to reassure my aunt that all was well.

That was one of the things I liked about Mr. Singh. He didn't badger me for details or complain about the distance. He simply got things done.

Meanwhile, I trotted back to Aunt Dee's, keeping an eye out for armed bogeymen hiding in bushes. Fortunately there were none, and I made it safely.

An hour later, filled to overflowing with tea and the most delicious cake I'd ever had, Mr. Singh arrived in Aunt Butty's motor, and I bid Phil and Aunt Dee a cheery goodbye with the promise to visit again. As long as there was cake, I'd go to the ends of the Earth.

Chapter 7

"Where to, my lady?" asked Mr. Singh once I was seated and he'd returned to his spot behind the wheel.

It was full dark by now. Much too late for any more questioning. Besides which, I desperately needed a stiff drink. "Back to the hotel, Mr. Singh."

"Very well." He did not so much as look at me sideways as he pulled out and motored down the street toward the hotel.

"Has my aunt been worried about me?"

"She has barely noticed you were gone. Too busy with her latest novel," he said. "What have you been up to?"

Now, in a butler, it was a very inappropriate question and one deserving of a dressing down, but in a partner, it wasn't entirely unexpected. I heaved a tired sigh. "If you must know, I was kidnapped."

He didn't make a sound, but one eyebrow went up.

"Yes, yes, I know. I am humiliated. I should have been more on guard."

"I suppose you will know better for next time." Was it me? Or was his tone drier than necessary?

"Hopefully there won't be a next time. I'm getting mightily tired of people poking me with revolver barrels. At least they didn't tie me up this time." I'd once had an American mobster do just that. It had been terribly exciting. Aunt Butty was with me. She still talks about it at every dinner party.

"Did this particular kidnapper explain why you were being kidnapped?" Mr. Singh asked.

"Not exactly." I told him about my abduction from the hotel, followed by Haigh's ordering me to back off. "I can only assume he was referring to our investigation, though I've no idea why."

"Perhaps we should drive there and confront him."

"By ourselves? I think not. They had guns, Mr. Singh. *Guns*. And it's getting a bit late. I am not fond of the idea of facing him in the middle of the night. Tomorrow we can confront Mr. Haigh en masse."

He nodded. "Very good. Have you any other plans for tomorrow?"

"Indeed. I wish to question Mildred Pierce. The groundskeeper at the Pavilion mentioned her."

We drove the rest of the way in silence, which was fine by me. Yes, there were things we probably needed to discuss about the case, but right now I needed to contemplate things in my own mind.

As we trundled down the road, I silently mulled over the events. I still was completely befuddled as to why I'd been kidnapped in the first place. I didn't actually *know* anything. And unfortunately, my abductors hadn't revealed anything of use.

Or had they?

"Mr. Singh, do you know a person called Haigh?"

"The name sounds familiar, but I cannot place it, my lady. I will give it some thought."

"Fair enough."

"Why do you ask?" He never took his eyes from the road.

"Apparently, that was the name of the man—I refuse to call him a gentleman, although he had a very nice house—who had me kidnapped. Mr. R Haigh. He only introduced himself by his surname, but I saw his first initial on an envelope on his desk. They left me alone in the library, you see."

"How very stupid of them." His tone was definitely dry this time.

"Yes, rather," I agreed. "So now I'm trying to think of who this mysterious R. Haigh is. What does the R stand for, do you suppose? Robert? Reginald?"

"Ralph," Mr. Singh suggested.

"Oh, good one. Rudolfo. Remington," I continued.

"Romeo. Rufus," Mr. Singh suggested, getting into the spirit of the game.

"Radcliffe," I offered. "Or Ragnar."

"Rafiq. Rajiv."

I laughed. "None of this is helping, is it?"

"It cheered you up, my lady."

He wasn't wrong there, and I had that sudden stab of realization that the day Aunt Butty met Mr. Singh had been a very lucky day for us all.

Upon arriving at the hotel, I went straight up to my room where I found Maddie in the midst of unpacking several suitcases.

"My lady!" She stared at me aghast. "Your dress! What have you done? Take it off this instant."

"Good gosh, you're a bossy one. Why did I bring you down from London again?"

She rolled her eyes. "Because you clearly cannot live without me. Here." She held out a clean dress. "Give me that one and I will attempt to rid it of mud. And your poor coat!"

"If you insist," I said, handing her my coat. "Did you speak to Hale before you left?"

"No, but I sent a note 'round. He sent this back." She handed me a rather rumpled envelope.

In the bathroom, which was appointed with all the mod cons, I finally got a good look at myself and realized how ghastly my appearance was. Mud streaked up one side of my dress. My hair was in a state, with bits sticking out at odd angles and a ball of moss caught up in one wave. My mascara had pooled under my eyes making me look like a raccoon and my lipstick had long worn off. I couldn't believe anyone had let me into their house looking like this. Either Phil and her aunt were half blind, or they were the kindest people on the planet.

Before anything else, I ripped open the envelope. Hale's bold handwriting sprawled in thick slashes across the page.

Dearest O,

I'm sorry I'm missing your latest adventure. Wish I could be there with you. Stay safe and I'll see you when you get back.

Love,

H

As love letters went, it wasn't exactly the most scintillating, but Hale showed his passion in other ways. I tucked it away in my makeup bag for safe keeping.

After a quick refresh and change into a clean peach dress and gold t-straps, I handed off the dirty one to Maddie who turned up her nose at the offending garment. However, I knew if anyone were able to restore it, she could. Hopefully she could save my coat, as well. It was a particular favorite of mine.

I made my way down stairs where the hotel's cocktail hour was in full swing. Waiters were circling the lobby with martini glasses of pink liquid. I snagged one and took a swig. It was oddly sweet and a bit sour at the same time. Very... pineapple-y.

"There you are, Ophelia. I wondered where you'd got to." Aunt Butty swanned up wearing a gold lame gown with a royal blue silk kimono covered in dragons over it. Her hair was done up in a matching gold and blue turban and massive coral earrings dangling from her lobes. "Aren't these cocktails marvelous? I could drink my weight in them."

"What are they, darling?"

"Mary Pickford. Not the actress. Named for her. I understand rum is involved, and I do love rum." She drained her glass and exchanged it for a full one from a passing waiter.

"What did you get up to this afternoon?" I asked casually.

"Had a hot toddy and read my book awhile. Then a lovely nap. You?" She eyeballed a distinguished looking older gentleman in a tailcoat.

"Well, while you were snoring the afternoon away, I was getting kidnapped."

She nearly sloshed her drink. "*What*?! Tell me everything."

I dragged her over near the fireplace where a fire was burning merrily. The warmth was most welcome. "After our jaunt, I stopped in the lobby to ring Louise."

"Go on."

"Well, she told me about a friend of hers who lives here in Brighton. She thought he might be able to help. Dominic Parlance is his name."

"Oh, I know Dom."

My eyes widened. "You do? Why didn't you mention him?"

"I had no idea he lived in Brighton. Last I'd heard he was off to the Americas to make his fortune." She frowned. "Or maybe that was Dimitri."

I tried desperately not to shake her and instead gave her a quick rundown of the day's events, from getting kidnapped to my visit with Phil and her aunt.

"Good heavens, you've been busy."

"Aren't you at all upset I was kidnapped?"

"Well, you got un-kidnapped, didn't you?" she pointed out. "No use crying over spilt milk and all." She drained her cocktail glass and looked around for another.

"I want you to go back with me."

"Back?" she asked vaguely as a waiter appeared to give her a fresh Mary Pickford.

"To the house where the kidnappers took me. To confront Haigh."

"Do you really think that's wise?"

"Probably not," I admitted.

"What about Mildred Pierce? Should we speak to her?" Aunt Butty said.

"Yes, of course, darling. Dom, too, but I want to know what the devil is going on first. I'm certain that my being kidnapped has something to do with Emily's death."

"But how did they—whoever *they* are—know we were looking into it?" she asked.

She made a good point. How indeed? "I don't know, but right now it's the best lead I've got."

Shéa MacLeod

Chapter 8

The next morning dawned bright and clear, though perhaps a bit soggy around the edges and definitely on the chilly side. I dressed in a simple blue merino wool with a matching hat Maddie had packed for me and a sensible pair of brown ankle boots. Better for running across muddy lawns, I suppose.

Aunt Butty had insisted on breakfast first, so over pots of coffee and tea and offerings of eggs benedict from the American chef—really, an America chef, who'd ever heard of such a thing? —we plotted our morning venture. Naturally, our plans involved Mr. Singh.

"I think we should just drive up, knock on the door, and demand to see this Mr. Haigh person," Aunt Butty said.

"Don't be daft, darling," I disagreed. "He's liable to shoot us. Or do something else equally disagreeable."

"What's as equally disagreeable as getting shot?" She genuinely wanted to know.

"I've no idea. But I'm sure there are plenty of unpleasant things he could do to us."

"That no doubt is true." She sliced off a large chunk of egg and bacon, swiped it through the rich, creamy hollandaise sauce and popped it in her mouth. "Goodness, this is marvelous."

"I think we should case the place first. Mr. Singh can help. He's very sneaky."

"That's certainly true," Aunt Butty agreed. "The man is half cat."

"So Mr. Singh can snoop around, make sure it's safe and then..."

"And then?" she prodded.

"I'm not sure. If Haigh's there, we confront him."

"If he's not?"

I shrugged and licked hollandaise sauce off my fork. "I guess we can break in and poke around a bit."

"You really have no respect for the law, do you?" There was no censure in her tone.

"Of course not. I come by it honestly." And I gave her a wink.

After breakfast, we rounded up Mr. Singh and Simon and laid out our plan. First, we would hit up the Haigh house. Then we would visit Mildred Pierce.

Within the hour, we were ensconced in Aunt Butty's motorcar, Simon at the wheel with Mr. Singh sitting ramrod straight next to him. Today's dastar was pavo blue. It suited him well.

"It's quite lovely," Aunt Butty said as we zipped through the countryside. "One forgets how *green* everything is when one is in London."

She wasn't wrong there. The English countryside never disappointed as far as lush greenness went, but I was happy enough to view it from the comfortable seat of Aunt Butty's vehicle. I'd no interest in mucking about in it. I'd done plenty of that the previous evening.

At last we pulled up to the great manor house where I'd been held captive. No one came at the sound of our arrival, nor did anyone answer the door despite incessant beating upon it.

"I'll poke around," Simon offered. "See if there's another way in."

"You go that way," Mr. Singh directed, pointing to the right. "And I will take the other side. Perhaps between us, we'll find something."

"I suppose Ophelia and I will cool our heels here," Aunt Butty said, sounding not at all upset. Instead—as the men poked about the bushes—she withdrew a flask from her massive handbag, took a swig, and handed it over. "Gin."

While I took my turn, she rummaged around and pulled out a package of boiled sweets. Rhubarb and custard, my favorites. We took turns swigging gin and sucking on the sweets, which created an odd but delightful blend of flavors in the mouth.

"You know," I said cheerfully, "this would make an excellent cocktail."

"Rhubarb custard sweets and gin?" She looked horrified.

"Well, not the sweets. But perhaps some rhubarb liquor and something... custard-like." I took another swallow of gin. "What sort of liquor tastes like custard?"

"Avocaat," she said promptly. "I had it in Germany once. 1890, I think it was. Somewhere in there. But they make it with brandy."

I blinked. "They make what with brandy?"

"Avocaat. You wanted a liquor that tasted like custard, well, that's what it is. Brandy, eggs, and sugar. Delightful stuff."

"I suppose one could use gin instead," I mused. "Then one just adds rhubarb liqueur and Bob's your uncle."

"I never did understand that saying," Aunt Butty said.

"What saying?"

"Bob's your uncle. I, for one, never had an uncle named Bob. I had an uncle Jim, but we don't like to talk about him."

I blinked. "It doesn't mean— oh, never mind." I shook my head. "What do you think about my cocktail idea?"

"Sounds delicious. We should try it sometime. I'm certain Mr. Singh can make it happen."

"If anyone can, it's Mr. Singh," I said, raising the flask.

Just then, Simon darted around the corner gesturing wildly. In a loud whisper he said, "My ladies! I've found it!"

We clambered out of the car and tiptoed after him, trying not to get our t-straps muddy. What he'd found was the coal shoot.

"I'm not going in there," I said stubbornly. "A window is one thing, but that..." I gestured. "If I get stuck, I'll never hear the end of it."

"Not to mention it would ruin that lovely dress." Aunt Butty drained the flask then stared at it with disappointment. "Bother."

"My ladies," a voice floated down from above.

The three of us craned our necks to see Mr. Singh's head sticking out of the window above us. Simon lifted his cap and scratched his head. "Well, I'll be."

"What are you doing up there, Mr. Singh?" Aunt Butty asked, her words a tad slurred.

"I picked the lock." He said it much as one might say, "I went to the opera" or "I had steak for dinner." The man was full of surprises.

"Jolly good!" Simon cheered. "That's a trick I could learn."

"We're coming in, Mr. Singh," I said. "Which door?"

"The French doors," he said. "The ones leading into the library."

The library where I'd been held hostage. "I know where it is." I led the way around the house, Simon and Aunt Butty following along like ducklings.

The French doors stood wide open and Aunt Butty's gaze went directly to the liquor cabinet. "I think I need a refill."

"You can't just steal someone's booze, Aunt Butty," I said, feeling like I should protest regardless of my own foray into the exact same cabinet during my previous visit.

"But of course I can. Besides, that man *kidnapped* you. The least he can do is donate a bit of gin to a good cause."

Turned out there wasn't any gin, so we left Aunt Butty to refill her flask with whiskey instead, and we joined Mr. Singh in the hall.

I hadn't had a good look at the place when I first arrived, being somewhat under duress at the time. I was impressed by the decor which was a mix of lovely antiques and light, bright fabrics in blues and yellows. It was sunny and warm. Not at all the sort of place one would have expected a thug like Mr. Haigh to reside.

"There's no one here at all?" I asked Mr. Singh. "Not even any staff?"

"No, my lady," he assured me. "Nearly all the rooms are covered in dust cloths and most of the shutters are locked. Only a few rooms appear to have been in any use recently."

"How dashed odd," I muttered. "I guess we're not confronting Mr. Haigh."

"Not today at any rate," Simon agreed cheerfully. "But we can still poke about, can't we? Maybe find out what the chappy is up to."

We split up with Simon heading downstairs to the kitchen and cellar, Mr. Singh taking the attic, and Aunt Butty and I prowling the rest of the house whilst simultaneously keeping an eagle eye out for encroachers (of which there were none). We all met back an hour later with Aunt Butty waving a framed photograph.

"This will help," she declared, shoving the thing at me.

I stared down at the image of a man who appeared to be his forties, clean shaven and good looking in a bland sort of way. He had a weak chin and eyes set just a smidge too close together, saving him from being actually handsome. "And how does this help?"

"Well, because we can show it to people. Ask around about him."

"Why would we ask around about this man?" I handed her back the photo.

"Because it's Mr. Haigh," she said.

I laughed. "No, it's not."

"Yes, it is. It was on Mrs. Haigh's nightstand. And see." She removed the photograph from the frame and thrust it at me. "Look at the back."

Sure enough, on the back was scrawled *Roland Haigh, Summer 1928*. So that was his name. "Well, this isn't the man I met."

"No?" She took the picture back and stuck it in the frame. "Are you certain?"

"Quite. The man I met was older, plumper, and had an enormous moustache. Not as... refined."

"So the man you met was an imposter," Mr. Singh mused.

"Why would he claim to be this Mr. Haigh if he weren't?" Simon wondered.

"Obviously so I wouldn't know his real name," I said. "And if I were to complain about it to the police, I'd look like a fool when they confronted the real Mr. Haigh."

"That does seem to be the case," Mr. Singh agreed.

"Question is, where is the real Mr. Haigh?" I mused. "Hopefully they haven't harmed him."

"I doubt that," Aunt Butty said. "According to the calendar I found in Mrs. Haigh's dressing room, they're off to Majorca for a month. That's why the house is shut up."

"Which means whoever kidnapped Lady R and brought her here knew they'd be gone," Simon said.

"Exactly," I agreed. "Which means whoever it is knows them. At least well enough to know they're out of town. I wonder who that could be? And what about the housekeeper? Was she the real one? Or someone brought in to playact?"

"Does it matter," Aunt Butty said. "You're safe now, and whoever that man was is long gone."

"I doubt he's gone far," Mr. Singh said. "I am certain he's involved in all this."

"I agree," I said. "We need to find out who he really is. If we can do that, then we might discover what this is all about and what he has to do with Emily."

"Very well," Aunt Butty said, striding for the library.

"Where are you going, darling?" I demanded. "We've got a lot of house left to search."

"No sense in it," she said, flapping her hand at me. "We're not going to find anything here. This was just a… stage. But Dom can help. We'll visit him after we pop in on Mildred Pierce."

I trotted after her, Mr. Singh and Simon hot on our heels. "You're sure he'll talk to us?"

Aunt Butty laid the photograph on the desk then paused at the doors. "Oh, yes. He's a good friend of mine. Or was, once upon a time. He knows everything there is to know about everyone in Brighton, but he doesn't get up until late afternoon."

"Of course, he doesn't," I muttered.

But she didn't hear me. She'd already slipped through the open door and disappeared from view.

We drew up in front of an English country cottage. It was one of those chocolate box type places with diamond paned windows, a low thatched roof, and thick white-washed walls. The door was painted forest green to match the shutters, and the front garden—though hardly bigger than a postage stamp—was a delightful jumble of plants, a few already blooming even this early in the year. I could tell that later on it would be a riot of color.

Mr. Singh led the way, rapping on the door before turning to me. "Perhaps I should wait in the car with Simon and your aunt."

Aunt Butty was well on her way to being thoroughly tipsy, so we'd left her in Simon's care while I confronted Mildred Pierce.

"Why? This is your investigation, too," I pointed out.

"It is unlikely Mildred Pierce will feel comfortable around me."

He meant because he was Indian. Because he wasn't white. Because my name would open doors that would only slam in his face. I felt a snap of anger at the unfairness of it. But before I could answer, the door swung open.

Mildred Pierce looked to be about a hundred. She was small, barely up to my bosom, and stoop-shouldered with a frizz of gray curls tucked into a messy bun, a face like wrinkled linen, and small, bright eyes that peered at us over half-moon glasses. "Yes?" She glanced from me to Mr. Singh with a puzzled expression.

"Mrs. Mildred Pierce?" I asked.

"Yes, dear. Only it's just Miss."

"I am Ophelia, Lady Rample. And this is Mr. Singh."

She blinked. "Good heavens. What is a proper lady doing at my humble cottage?"

"I met the groundskeeper up at the Pavilion earlier and she said you might be able to answer some questions we had about the time when it was a hospital."

Her eyes widened. "Oh, were you there, dear?" She looked directly at Mr. Singh.

"Yes, madam."

"Well, don't just stand there. Come in. Come in."

She led us into a small parlor overfilled with heavy Victorian furniture to the point one could barely move. It was a bit musty smelling and chilly, but otherwise quite neat and clean, if overstuffed. I perched on an armchair chair whilst Mr. Singh remained standing, clearly uncomfortable in any role but his chosen one of butler.

"I'll be back with a nice pot of tea." And without waiting for our answer, Mildred Pierce trundled out of the room.

I would have much preferred something stronger. Or to skip it altogether and get straight to the point. But the niceties must be observed.

After what seemed an age, she finally returned, tea tray in hand, the teapot rattling so fiercely I was afraid she was ready to drop the thing. Mr. Singh quickly rescued it from her.

She beamed at him. "What a nice young man. Set it there, and I'll pour."

He placed it gently on the indicated surface which happened to be a rather stodgy side table. She slopped some tea into a cup and handed it to me. No milk or sugar. Not even lemon. Was she forgetful? Or perhaps strapped? The tea was weak and somehow bitter at the same time, but I managed to choke some down.

"Now, you wanted to know about the time when the Pavilion was a hospital," she said, handing Mr. Singh a cup before taking a sip of her own tea and smacking her lips in delight. "Oh, that were a time. All those soldiers about… so handsome in their uniforms. I went to all the dances. I was much younger then, you see. I though perhaps I could finally catch myself a husband. Alas, it wasn't to be!"

I didn't say anything. The poor woman had to have been eighty even then. Well, perhaps seventy.

"I used to go up to the hospital and read to the troops. The ones who couldn't do for themselves. So far from home, poor lads—"

"Mrs. Pierce," I finally interrupted, "what I really want to know is, do you remember when that nurse went missing?"

"Emily? But of course. It was in all the papers. Oh, not right when she went missing. But when they found her. Poor little thing. Drowned herself."

"Did she?" I shot Mr. Singh a glance, but he was as impassive as a glacier.

"That's what they said, and why would they lie?"

"Why, indeed? Did you know her?"

Her gaze went oddly shrewd. "Why do you ask, dear?"

"Because you called her Emily," I said. "Not Miss Pearson or Nurse Emily, but just Emily."

She chuckled. "Caught me out. Like I said, I used to volunteer, you see, up at the hospital. Cleaning. Making tea. Reading to the boys. That sort of thing. Some of the nurses were right uppity madams, but Emily, she was kind. Terribly kind. Even to those as might not have deserved it."

"What do you mean by that?" I asked, watching her closely.

"Just not that everyone deserved her kindness." She took a prim sip of her tea. "And I'm not talking about the patients."

"Are you talking about the doctors?" I prodded.

"Doctors. Nurses. There were some there as didn't deserve so much as a smile from her."

Was she being deliberately vague? Somehow, I didn't think so. I decided to switch tactics. "You became friends?"

"Of a sort. Work colleagues I think you'd say now. We took our tea together sometimes. Chatted about this and that. Hospital gossip."

My ears perked up. "What sort of gossip?"

"You know the sort, which doctor is getting a little too friendly with which nurse. Which cook waters down the soup. Which patient is being sent back to the Front." Her eyes sparkled, as if even now she got a little thrill from the memory of gossiping with Emily.

"What about Emily herself? Did you find out much about her?"

"Oh, a little. Not much. She wasn't one to talk about herself." Mrs. Pierce took a delicate sip of tea. "I always thought she was a little shy."

I thought she was telling the truth. "What do you remember?"

"Well, I remember her people came from some village or other over West. Near Salisbury, I believe. But she loved Brighton and had decided to stay even after the war. Had a little place in Market Street above a shop. Not far from India Gate. Had a fella, too."

"Did she." I was nervous all of a sudden. I wasn't sure Mr. Singh wanted anyone knowing of his relationship with Emily.

"Sure enough. Talked about him all the time. Never did tell me who he was, though."

I could almost feel Mr. Singh's relief as if it were my own. I smiled at Mrs. Pierce. "That's very interesting, but it would be more interesting if you remembered the name of the village she was from or specifically which flat in Brighton she lived in."

"I believe the village was Stonebury. No, wait…Netherbridge." She rubbed her forehead. "Oh, dear, that doesn't seem right, does it? I'm afraid my memory isn't what it was."

I gave her a warm smile, despite being disappointed. "Don't worry. It's not that important." I wasn't sure that was true, but I didn't want her to feel bad. "What about a nurse named Dorothy Evans? Did you know her?"

She frowned thoughtfully. "The name is familiar, but I can't recall which one she was. There were so many of them, you see. So many young things pressed into service."

I decided to try one more time. "Are you sure you can't remember any gossip Emily might have told you? Perhaps something that might have to do with why she disappeared?"

"Well, I don't know that it had anything to do with her disappearance," she said, then paused.

Mr. Singh and I both leaned forward. I don't know if he was holding his breath, but I knew I was.

"Yes?' I prodded.

"One evening I remember her saying something about there being not enough morphine."

I sat back. "What did she mean by that?"

"I'm not certain," she admitted. "But more than once she claimed there was less of something than there should be."

"Other than just the morphine?" I asked.

"Oh, yes. I don't recall everything, but I know she complained fairly often about not having enough supplies. Medicines usually. I always thought it was odd."

"Why odd?" I asked.

"You see, they made that place a hospital for the Indian soldiers because it *looked* rather like something from India. They wanted them to feel at home. To feel cared for so they would want to keep fighting for the Empire. Clever if you ask me. They even divided up the wards depending on where the soldiers came from and had special cooks for each ward to make just the right kind of food."

I turned to Mr. Singh who nodded and spoke for the first time. "I am from Punjab originally. I can attest that the ward where I stayed had an excellent Punjabi cook."

"Were you there?" Mildred asked.

He bowed. "Yes, madame. I had that honor."

She sighed. "It was a wonderful hospital. That's why I was so confused about Emily's claims. It was so well equipped, and they put such care into every little detail, that to run short on basic medicines?" She shook her head. "Near the end of the war, they did run short, but then there should have been plenty."

Alas, that proved to be all she could tell us, and Mr. Singh and I left only marginally more informed than when we went in.

Chapter 9

Aunt Butty's friend was not at all what I expected.

Being in my aunt's circle—not to mention being a friend of Louise Pennyfather's—I expected someone who was an Original. Possibly exotic. Probably Bohemian. Definitely different in the best possible way. But Dominic Parlance was like no one I'd ever met in my life.

Aunt Butty led us to a small cafe on a narrow backstreet in Brighton. It was a very French sort of place complete with violin music, red-flocked wallpaper, and dark wood furniture. It was completely empty save a woman sitting at a corner table in the back. She rose as we approached, and I found myself staring up and up in something approaching awe.

She was well over six feet tall to begin with, but her heels made her even taller. Her dark auburn hair was fashionably cut with straight bangs and little waves around her ears. Perfectly penciled eyebrows and thin lips painted in rich red set off with the hint of a dimple in the chin. She was neatly dressed in a chocolate brown rayon dress and a simple locket necklace. Her hands were covered in matching chocolate brown gloves. Nothing flashy, and yet her presence was palpable. She was a formidable woman.

"Butty! How delightful to see you." The voice was definitely not that of a woman, but a deep, masculine base.

I blinked, stunned at first, then fascinated. I'd heard of men who preferred to dress as women. People whispered about them as if there was something shocking and wrong with them and they ought to be put away for the good of society. I wasn't sure exactly how this was supposed to be for society's good. Frankly, I thought a person ought to be able to dress as they liked and hang the world. But I did wonder why a person would choose to wear stockings over trousers if they didn't have to.

"Dominic!" my aunt crowed. "It's been an age."

There were hugs and cheek kisses and mutual delight in each other's appearance.

"How is dear Louise?" Dominic asked at last.

"Marvelous," Aunt Butty said. "Her husband just bought he a diamond necklace and she's over the moon. This is my niece, Ophelia, Lady Rample. Ophelia, this is my dear friend, Dominic Parlance."

"Pleased to meet you," I said, offering my hand politely.

Instead I found myself engulfed in a massive hug redolent of Vol de Nuit. "Dear girl,"—Dominic said it "gel"—"how lovely to finally meet you!"

"You, as well, Miss Parlance."

Dominic let out a bark of laughter. "Just Dom, darling. Nothing fancy." Rings flashed on Dom's fingers. Clearly not one for subtlety.

"Ophelia." I smiled.

Dom gave me the once-over in a way I was very used to receiving from men. "Aren't you a peach of a thing."

I lifted a brow. "As are you." Dom did look rather fetching.

"Stop flirting with my niece, Dom," Aunt Butty snapped.

"But she's just my type, doll. And by that, I mean rich." Dom gave me a wink, and I laughed.

"Dom fancies himself a ladies' man," Aunt Butty growled. "Only the ladies won't have him."

"It's true," Dom admitted cheerfully. "Something about me being prettier."

"Oh. I see." I wasn't sure what to say. I'd assumed that, like Chaz, Dom had other preferences.

Dom snickered. "I doubt that, doll. I may like dressing as a woman, but I also prefer women. I'm open, mind you. Never like to miss out on a good thing, but preferences are what they are, darling. Don't you think?"

"Er, rather." Dom's frankness was both alarming and refreshing.

"Usually I wouldn't be so open with a stranger, but seeing as how you're Butty's niece, I can't imagine anything would shock or horrify you terribly much."

"I once saw my aunt skinny dipping in a duck pond," I said. "So, no. Not much shocks me."

"I'll have you know I look good naked. For a woman my age," Aunt Butty protested.

"It's true, darling," I admitted. "But you were skinny dipping with Louise Pennyfather who, while a marvelous human being, does not at all look good naked for a woman of her or any other age."

"Louise may be my best friend," Aunt Butty said, "but she does look like an old leather handbag, God love her."

Dom let out a very masculine guffaw and waved at the barman. "Poor Louise. She never was a looker, but she is fierce, and I admire her thoroughly. Round of drinks for my friends."

"What are we drinking?" I asked.

"Ward 8, doll. I hope you like rye whiskey."

"Do I ever!" I grinned.

With efficient movements, the barman poured rye whiskey into a shaker along with orange and lemon juices and grenadine. He shook it vigorously so that the ice rattled around delightfully, then poured it into three cocktail glasses, added maraschino cherries, and served them with a flourish.

"Oh, well done!" Dom clapped enthusiastically before lifting a glass. "Chin-chin, girls!"

"Chin-chin," we echoed.

The cocktail was surprisingly sour, but not unpleasantly so. I wouldn't have minded a bit more grenadine.

"Now, tell me what you dames need from little ole me," Dom said, setting the cocktail glass neatly on the bar.

"Do you know a gentleman named Roland Haigh?" Aunt Butty asked.

"But of course, doll. Regular visitor of the theater. Sometimes with his wife. Sometimes not so much." A brow waggle gave meaning to Dom's inference. "Nice man. Lives in an old pile out in the country. How do you know him?"

"We don't," I said. "He kidnapped me."

Dom's red-painted lips rounded. "Well I never!"

"Only it wasn't actually this Haigh person," Aunt Butty explained. "It was some other man who claimed to be Haigh."

Dom frowned. "How baffling."

"Indeed," I agreed. "We have no idea who the man is who actually kidnapped me, but we figure it had to be someone who knew Haigh well enough to know he would be away for some time and his house would be empty."

"I thought you might have some idea who that could be," Aunt Butty continued.

"Well, just about everyone, I'd say," Dom mused. "I mean, it's common knowledge among theater people that Roland Haigh goes to Spain this time of year for a few weeks. It's pretty much the only time he ever misses a play."

"Theater people," I echoed.

"Yes, that's pretty much who he spends his time with when he's not in London on business or being dragged about to boring house parties by his wife. We might not know specific dates or the details of his household, but we know when he's gone, that's where he's off to."

Aunt Butty and I exchanged looks.

"Are there any particular theater people he's closer to than others?" I asked. "Ones who might know more about the workings of his household?"

Dom twisted the stem of the cocktail glass between gloved fingers. "Let me think... I know he spends a great deal of time around Molly Malloy. Positively smitten with her, if I'm honest."

"I bet John Goode doesn't like that," Aunt Butty muttered.

"Not particularly," Dom agreed. "Rather jealous, that one."

"Jealous enough he might want to get back at Mr. Haigh by using his empty house as a crime scene?" I asked. I knew Goode hadn't posed as Mr. Haigh or any of the henchmen, but that didn't mean he hadn't set it up.

Dom's perfectly penciled eyebrows shot up. "I wouldn't have thought so. He's such a quiet man, Mr. Goode, but still waters run deep and all that. One never knows, do they?"

No. One never did.

An idea sparked. "Have you heard of a nurse named Emily Pearson? She worked up at the Pavilion during the war."

"Of course, darling. Everyone has. Ghastly what happened to her." Dom gave me a look. "Why do you ask?"

"A friend of ours was very close to her," Aunt Butty explained. "We're trying to find out what happened to her."

"He doesn't think she drowned herself," Dom guessed. "Or that it was an accident."

"Indeed, not," I affirmed. "And based on what's been happening, I'm starting to think it wasn't either."

"Well, I don't know much," Dom admitted. "I never met her personally, you see, but I do recall there was a secret man in her life. Great hullabaloo over that, though they never figured out who the fellow was."

I didn't mention that we did know who the fellow was. Instead I asked, "I don't suppose you ever heard who her friends were? Where she came from?"

"I haven't a clue who her friends were," Dom said. "But if I recall, the paper said she came from Netherstone."

Netherstone was a good two hour drive away, so we headed out the next morning fresh as proverbial daisies and loaded down with picnic baskets provided by the hotel at Aunt Butty's insistence. Not that it was picnicking weather, but it was best to be prepared. All I cared about were the two bottles of champagne in the hampers.

Simon drove at an easy pace through the rolling countryside. Mr. Singh sat beside him, straight as a rod, face expressionless, but I could swear I felt his nervousness.

Was that even possible? Did the indomitable Mr. Singh get nervous?

We passed through numerous chocolate box villages, crossed over more than one stone bridge so narrow the Bentley barely squeezed through, and saw more sheep than people. Daffodils nodded along hedgerows and forsythia added a splash of bright color here and there. The world was slick and wet from last night's rain and when I rolled down the window, the air was redolent of petrichor and fresh, blooming things.

Simon let out a tremendous sneeze.

"Bless you, dear," Aunt Butty said automatically.

"Thanks, milady. Sorry 'bout that. Always get a bit sniffly this time of year," he said apologetically.

I rolled up the window, abashed. Poor Simon.

At last we reached the village of Netherstone. Aunt Butty eyed it askance, while I felt a stab of disappointment.

"This is it?" I suppose I'd expected another darling village tucked among the green hills of England. Thatched roofs and weathervanes and all that.

Netherstone could barely be called a village. Hardly bigger than a hamlet, it boasted a church so tiny as to be no more than a chapel and a single pub which looked to be located in the front room of someone's home and held the dubious moniker of the Three-Legged Donkey. It was as if someone got tired of driving over to the next village for a pint and figured they'd make a bit of extra income by inviting their neighbors around to their parlor for a pint and charging them for the pleasure. Around those were perhaps half a dozen or so cottages, all of which had seen better days.

"Emily grew up here?" I mused aloud. "No wonder she got out as soon as she could."

"She did say that living in such a small village was difficult for her," Mr. Singh agreed.

"Everyone up in everyone else's business," Simon agreed. Being from a small village himself, he ought to know. "Good for us though."

He had a point. In a place like this, everyone knew everything about everyone else. If only we could get them to talk. Too bad Chaz wasn't here. He could charm state secrets out of the Pope.

"Which house was hers, do you suppose?" Aunt Butty mused, eyeballing the small collection of homes.

"I could ask at the pub," Simon offered. "Though it doesn't seem open."

Mr. Singh pointed. "That one."

It was, perhaps, the smallest of all the cottages and had been more recently white-washed, although it was still a bit on the dingy side. The shutters and doors were a faded tomato red, unlike the other houses which sported blue, green, or plain brown. A plethora of windchimes hung from the eaves, tinkling in the light breeze.

"Are you certain, Mr. Singh?" Aunt Butty asked.

He was not offended, although he probably should have been. Mr. Singh was never uncertain about anything as far as I could tell. "Yes, my lady. She spoke often of her mother's love for windchimes."

There were certainly a lot of them, and none of the other houses had any.

"Well, then, we best be getting on with it." Without waiting for Simon or Mr. Singh, Aunt Butty heaved herself from the car and strode toward the cottage.

I scurried after her, curious about what we would find. Would Emily's mother still be alive, living in the same little cottage? Would she even want to speak to two strange women?

Aunt Butty rapped on the door with the handle of her umbrella. We waited for what seemed ages, listening to the tinkling of the nearest windchime. There wasn't a sound from inside and the place had a sort of deserted air about it. As if its inhabitants had gone away and meant to come back but forgotten somehow.

Aunt Butty rapped again.

"If you're lookin' for Mrs. Pearson, you've missed her. She's gone." The next-door neighbor leaned on the rather rickety fence hat tilted back on his balding head. He eyed us carefully with watery eyes, but there was nothing of suspicion or distrust about him. Merely curiosity.

"When will she come back?" Aunt Butty asked.

"You misunderstand me," he said. "She's *gone.* Buried her over at the church a month ago."

"Oh, that's dreadful. I am so sorry," she gushed.

I echoed her sentiments, disappointed that we'd hit a dead end. We seemed to be running into a lot of those.

"Poor woman just never was right after that daughter of hers up and died," he said.

"Yes, that's why we came," Aunt Butty said. "My niece here was good friends with Emily during the war. Since we were in the area, we wanted to visit Mrs. Pearson."

"Ah, she'd have loved that. Didn't get many visitors after Emily died. Not even sure where the house goes." He shrugged as if to say it wasn't his problem.

"Many?" I echoed.

"Eh?" He blinked at me.

"You said she didn't get *many* visitors. Which means she must have got some," I pointed out.

His expression brightened as if thrilled to impart a tidbit of gossip. "Oh, aye. Was a man who used to come once in a blue moon. Roll up in a fancy car, go in for a few minutes, then leave. Very strange."

"Why's that?" Aunt Butty asked.

He scratched his head. "Well, now, nobody knew who he was, and she would never say. Which was odd in and of itself. But every time he came, she would cry. Now what sort of man makes a woman cry like that, I ask you? And a widow what's lost her only child to boot."

We murmured that, indeed, it wasn't much of a man to do that. But it did make me wonder. Fancy car. A man no one knew. Could it be someone trying to cover up Emily's murder?

"When was the last time this man came?" I asked.

"Don't rightfully recall," he admitted, "but it weren't more'n a month or two before her death."

Which meant no more than two or three months prior. "What did he look like?"

The neighbor scratched his arm. "Well, now, that's a pickle. Just plain. Ordinary. A little on the small side." His eyes widened. "And he had a scar." He traced his cheek in the exact spot where the driver of the car that kidnapped me had a scar.

My heart thudded wildly. "And do you remember what sort of car he was driving?"

"Sure. It were dark gray. Big thing. Had those double Rs on the front. Real fancy with red seats and all."

"Rolls Royce?" I squeaked.

"That's the one."

So Mrs. Pearson's mysterious visitor had to be very wealthy indeed. Why would a man who drove a Rolls Royce visit Emily's mother for years after her death?

Aunt Butty gripped my wrist. "I know that car," she hissed. Louder she said, "Thank you, Mr...?"

"Johnson," he said with a grin. "And feel free to stop by any time."

He went back to his gardening and we scuttled back to the car.

"Back to Brighton, Simon," my aunt ordered. "We need to speak to a man about a car."

"Who is it, Aunt Butty? Who are we going to see?" I demanded once we were all seated and the car was on its way back to Brighton.

"You recall the actress we saw on the train?"

"Of course. Molly Malloy."

"And the man she was with?"

"John Goode."

She nodded grimly.

"*He* owns the car?" I asked, astonished.

"Or one very like it."

I gripped the door handle. "But it wasn't John Goode that Johnson described."

"Oh, right. Who was it, then?"

"It was the man who was driving the vehicle the night I was kidnapped," I protested. Besides, I thought Goode was a low-level government official. How could he possibly own such a car?"

"And how could he afford to stay at the grandest hotel in the city?" she countered.

"I thought we'd decided that was down to Molly," I reminded her.

"Perhaps," she said thoughtfully, "but I recall once upon a time there were certain rumors..."

My eyes widened. "What sort of rumors?"

"The sort that, if true, could send a man to prison for a very long time."

Chapter 10

Neither John Goode nor Molly Malloy were at the hotel when we arrived back. "Gone to the theater," the desk clerk informed us. "Miss Malloy is performing tonight."

"Then I will take two tickets to her performance," Aunt Butty declared.

"Three," I corrected. "Mr. Singh will no doubt want to join us."

The clerk gaped like a fish. "I'm sorry, my ladies, but the performance has been sold out for weeks."

Aunt Butty rummaged in her reticule and pulled out a five pound note. "Pity. This was about to find a new home." She waved it in his face.

"I-I'll see what I can do," he stammered, picking up the telephone.

"Do you suppose we have time to go for a drink?" I muttered.

"Best not. Out of sight, out of mind. And I intend to stay front and center in that boy's mind until he has procured the tickets."

And so we stood there rather awkwardly in the lobby of the hotel, waiting on the poor man who looked increasingly nervous. But at last he rang off and waved us over.

"I was able to get you into the wings backstage. I know it's not proper seats, but—"

"We'll take it!" Aunt Butty declared.

He nearly wilted in relief. "Go to the stage door and ask for Mr. Butcher. He'll let you in."

"You see what you can get done when you put your mind to it, Ophelia?"

"Or your money," I said dryly.

It wasn't raining, so we didn't bother disturbing Simon. Instead, we changed into flashier gowns—mine was a lovely dove-gray silk in a Grecian style and Aunt Butty's a rather more startling canary yellow—and traipsed down the hill to the theater, Mr. Singh following along grimly. I wasn't entirely sure he was thrilled about spending the evening watching a play, but he was determined to join our little adventure if it meant learning the truth about Emily.

The stage door was down an alley, but at least it was well lit and surprisingly clean. I only have a passing acquaintance with alleys, but the last one I was in was dank and smelled of rotting rubbish. Most unpleasant.

Aunt Butty rapped at the door and it swung open, revealing a man who barely came up to my bosom. He had a shock of red hair and a luxurious red moustache. "Yes?"

"We are here for Mr. Butcher," Aunt Butty said.

He eyed Mr. Singh looming behind us. "That's me. You the fancy lady from the hotel?"

Fancy lady sounded rather dodgy, but Aunt Butty merely smiled and said, "Yes."

"Come on then." He shoved the door open wide so we could enter.

Inside, the air was redolent of dust and greasepaint and cheap perfume. Next to the door was a small counter behind which sat a chair. Mr. Butcher collected a mug from the counter and took a sip, made a face. "Tea's gone cold." He eyeballed us as if somehow the shortcomings of his tea were our fault.

We followed him through a narrow hall, dimly lit, passing doors open to dressing and storage rooms filled with props and costumes. Two scantily dressed women hurried by, chattering about their lines and how divine somebody looked in his costume.

I glanced behind to see Mr. Singh's reaction. He was pointedly ignoring the theater girls.

We passed a railing filled with costumes of all sorts and colors. A rather plain middle-aged woman was pulling a satin cape from the rack. When she caught sight of us, she dropped the cape and quickly bent to pick it up. I felt as if I'd seen her somewhere but couldn't quite place her.

Up a set of stairs we went onto what I supposed was the back of the stage. He led us to what was clearly the wings where someone had set up two comfortable looking armchairs. The curtain mostly blocked our view of the seats, but we'd a good view of the stage which had been carefully staged to look like the parlor of a great house.

"Here you go," Butcher said with a nod. "Sorry, I didn't expect three of you."

"I will stand," Mr. Singh said gravely.

Butcher shrugged. "Do what suits you. But don't talk during the play, or everyone and their mother can hear you."

"Do you know John Goode?" Aunt Butty asked as she and I took our seats while Mr. Singh took his place behind us.

Mr. Butcher grimaced. "Sure. Spends half his time backstage with Miss Malloy. Some sort of toff. Too good for the likes of us."

Aunt Butty thanked him, and he wandered off to either procure fresh tea or return to his station, it was unclear which. Maybe both. We turned our attention to the stage.

The play was actually quite amusing if a tad on the racy side. Molly Malloy did an excellent job, and I could see why the play had been sold out. I couldn't help but wish Chaz was there. He'd have enjoyed it immensely and we'd have had a grand time chatting about it after.

But Chaz wasn't there, and Aunt Butty was on a mission. The minute the play was over, she got up and we marched to the dressing rooms. Molly's was easy enough to spot as it had a giant yellow star painted on the door.

"I will wait in the hall," Mr. Singh said once he sussed my aunt's intention. "Perhaps I can overhear something of interest amongst the other thespians."

In typical Aunt Butty fashion, she didn't bother to knock but charged straight in. The upside of this—or the downside, depending on how one looks at it—was we caught Molly Malloy in a rather intimate embrace with a man who was definitely *not* John Goode. In fact, he looked suspiciously like the gentleman playing the villain in the play we'd just seen.

Miss Malloy, barely dressed in some sort of feathery negligee, didn't have the grace to blush. Instead, she gave us a haughty look and refused to release the gentleman from her clutches. "This ain't the bathroom, Toots." Her verbiage was American, but her accent was pure East End.

"We aren't looking for the cloakroom," Aunt Butty said in her haughtiest lady-of-the-manor tone, looking down her rather long nose. "We are looking for Mr. Goode."

"Well, he ain't here, as you can see."

Again, gun moll language, East End voice. It was such a strange dichotomy.

"We were told he would be here," I said evenly. "So we'll wait." And I deliberately took a seat on the chaise longue against one wall. It was half piled with clothes, but there was enough room to sit.

Aunt Butty took the only armchair and propped her feet comfortably up on the footstool. "Yes, it's quite cozy here. We'll wait."

Miss Malloy let out an annoyed sigh. "Sorry, Edgar. Guess I'm busy. Get on with you."

He made as if to protest, but the look she gave him was hard enough to cut glass. He dutifully exited the dressing room, although he cast a last, longing look at his lady love. He must not mind sharing. I wondered if Goode felt the same.

Molly slouched on the seat of her dressing table and unscrewed the lid on one of the many glass pots. "Now, why are you two annoying me? Can't you see I'm busy?"

"Quite," Aunt Butty said tartly. "I don't know how you have the time."

Molly eyeballed my aunt. "What do you mean, ducks?"

"I mean, between keeping your two boyfriends happy—is it just the two? —and your career going, why I wonder you have any time left."

Molly threw back her head and laughed. For a brief moment, I had a sense of deja vu. I could have sworn I'd heard that laugh before. I gave a mental headshake. Probably it was because I'd seen Malloy on the stage before. Yes. That was likely it.

"Oh, I've got time, ducks," Molly said. "I've got all the time in the world. But that doesn't explain what you're doing here."

"Does John Goode know you're two-timing him?" I asked, more curious than anything.

"We got what they call an understanding, see? He don't ask me questions about my gentlemen friends, and I don't ask questions about whatever he gets up to."

"Perfectly understandable," Aunt Butty said. "Seeing as what he's up to involves kidnapping and murder."

Molly dropped her pot and cold cream exploded out, splatting against the mirror and her negligee. She glared at us in the mirror crossly. "Now see what you made me do."

"Don't play innocent," I said. "I bet you know all about what Mr. Goode gets up to. His illegal activities."

She lifted her chin. "I most certainly do not. Having a piece on the side is one thing. But I don't get involved in murder. Who's he supposed to have killed anyway?"

"Have you ever heard of a young woman named Emily Pearson?" Aunt Butty asked.

Molly frowned prettily and went back to smearing cold cream on her face. "Can't say as I have, ducks."

It seemed to me she was telling the truth, but it's hard to tell with theater types. I did find it a little odd she was perfectly willing to answer our questions rather than call Mr. Butcher to have us thrown out. I supposed that meant she'd nothing to hide. Still, I had more questions. "What about Mr. Goode's car?"

She shrugged. "What about it?"

"Well, how can he afford it? He's a low-level bureaucrat," I pointed out. "He doesn't make that much."

"No idea. Never thought to ask. I just figured he inherited it. The money, I mean."

"He didn't," Aunt Butty said. "So he has a great deal of money?"

"Depends on what you mean by a 'great deal,'" Molly said, wiping at the cold cream with a cloth. "Enough he takes me to the best clubs in London. And there was that trip to France last year. Oh, and First-Class tickets on the Pullman. Swanky."

"He paid for that?" I asked. We'd been certain she was the one paying for everything.

"I sure didn't. I do okay, but not that good. At least not from acting, if you know what I mean."

I did. She meant her various boyfriends, such as John Goode, paid her way most of the time. Not a bad gig if you didn't mind putting up with the foibles of a whole lot of men.

"Where is Mr. Goode?" Aunt Butty said. "We were told he'd be here tonight."

"Oh, he was, ducks, but he had to go running back to London. Some work emergency or other."

Aunt Butty and I exchanged glances. What work emergency could a low-level government worker who awarded contracts possibly have? It looked like we'd be headed back to London.

We arrived back in London late that evening. It was already dark out, and a fine drizzle washed the city into shimmering pools. I turned my collar to the chill, damp air and followed Aunt Butty's sashaying form into the cab. Mr. Singh sat up front with the cabbie, who gave him the side-eye, but was wisely silent.

Maddie had driven up with Simon in the car, along with our luggage. No doubt he had already dropped Maddie off and was safely ensconced in Aunt Butty's flat with a hot toddy and a warm fire.

Yes, I was envious. For instead of enjoying such a pleasant evening myself, I was forced to track down John Goode with my aunt and Mr. Singh.

"Surely it can wait until tomorrow," I'd protested.

"No indeed. What if he gets wind of our inquiries and flees the city? Something tells me that Malloy woman has a big mouth," Aunt Butty had said.

I'd a feeling Goode was already well aware of our inquiries. In fact, I was beginning to suspect he was somehow behind all this. I just wasn't sure why.

"It's hardly the done thing to call on a single gentleman at his home," I insisted.

Aunt Butty snorted. "Since when did the done thing ever stop you?"

She had me there, so I went along meekly. Well, perhaps not meekly, but I decided cooperation was the better part of valor. And once Mr. Singh decided to join us, I had no argument left.

We pulled up to the building where John Goode lived, and I immediately spotted something familiar. "Look! There's the car! The one the kidnappers were driving."

"Are you certain, my lady?" Mr. Singh asked, glancing over his shoulder.

"Most definitely," I assured him.

"Yes," Aunt Butty said grimly. "That's Goode's car. I'd know it anywhere."

I paid the driver and the three of us clambered out of the cab. The minute he drove off, we hustled across the street to peer into the car. Aunt Butty yanked open the door and we inspected the inside. Nothing at all to indicate it had been involved in my kidnapping. But I knew it was the car, although Goode had most definitely not been the one driving, nor had he been my kidnapper.

I shut the door carefully, not wanting someone to hear it and peek out a window. It would be tough to explain why we were poking about in someone else's car. "Now what?"

"Upstairs to Goode's flat, of course," Aunt Butty said.

There was no doorman, and Molly Malloy had given us his flat number—3C—so we sailed in and straight to the elevator. Which was, alas, out of service. And so we trudged up four flights of stairs, puffing away like steam engines. Or rather, Aunt Butty and I puffed. Mr. Singh wasn't even winded. Really, I should get myself in better shape if I was going to make a habit of this nonsense.

At last, Aunt Butty rapped on the door to 3C. There was no answer. She rapped again, and I pressed my ear to the door. Not a peep.

"Now what?" I asked.

She jiggled the door handle. "Locked." Her tone exuded disgust. "Can you pick it, Mr. Singh?"

He bowed. "Of course. If Lady Rample will loan me a hairpin."

I removed a hairpin from my coiffure and Mr. Singh got to work. Chaz had taught me the fine art of lock picking. I'd no idea where he'd learned it, but he was a dab hand at it, that's for certain. I was not nearly as talented, which meant it took quite a long time. I was glad we had Mr. Singh with us.

It took him but a few moments, in which I was certain we'd be caught out any second, but within short order Mr. Singh had the door open and we got our first look at Goode's rooms. I was utterly disappointed.

John Goode might drive a fancy car, but his digs were ridiculously small. A studio flat with a single bed in one corner behind a Chinese paper screen, a hot plate and sink as an excuse for a kitchen, and a single table and chair. No comfortable divan or even a wing-backed chair. And to say the place was slovenly was being kind. There were clothes everywhere and dirty dishes piled in the sink.

Mr. Singh opened a couple of cupboards before shaking his head. Meanwhile, I peeked under the bed and inside the drawer of the nightstand. Nothing.

"Surely he doesn't entertain his mistress here," Aunt Butty said, aghast. She'd found a bottle of something and was refilling her flask.

"Maybe they meet at a hotel," I suggested, ignoring her theft of Goode's liquor. "This is the sort of place one would expect someone of his income to live."

"I don't buy it. I bet he has another place outside London where no one will notice. Something posh. This is just for appearances."

She may be right about that. "In any case, I don't see any clues here."

"Indeed not. Onward!" And she sailed from the room, Mr. Singh close behind.

I followed, making sure to lock the door carefully behind. No sense alerting Goode that we'd broken in.

As we descended the never-ending stairs, I hoped this would be the end of it and I would be allowed to return home, kick off my shoes, and have that hot toddy by the fire. Getting kidnapped really takes it out of a person. Not to mention I missed Hale. Although he was no doubt playing a gig at the club tonight.

"Mr. Singh," Aunt Butty said, "you should go home."

"My lady—"

She waved him off. "Right now, we're just going for drinks. There's no sense you staying up late for nothing."

It took some doing, but she finally convinced him. The minute he was out of sight she turned to me. Her next words despoiled me of any notion I'd be allowed to go home soon. "We need to track that man down quickly," Aunt Butty said.

"Goode? How? We know nothing about him. And you just got rid of the one person who had the skills to help up find him."

"Pish posh. Where we're going, he would feel terribly out of place."

I stared at her. "What do you mean?"

"You know someone who knows a lot about everyone. Someone who can help us find Goode a lot faster than Mr. Singh can."

"Chaz is probably at a party or a club by now." She was right. Nightclubs weren't Mr. Singh's scene.

She sniffed. "Far too early. He's likely barely out of bed. Let's drop 'round."

"I'm sure he'll be thrilled," I said dryly.

"At the very least, we'll get a drink out of it," she said. "I'm positively gasping."

"You and me both."

Chapter 11

Chaz lived in a lovely Art Deco building not far away. Fortunately, *his* lift was in working order, so we arrived at his door without the huffing and puffing of the previous call.

He opened the door on the third knock, wearing a frown and his shirtsleeves. He was clearly in the midst of readying himself for a night on the town.

"Ophelia! Aunt Butty! Whatever are you doing here?" He kissed each of our cheeks as we entered.

"Don't you look swell?" I said as I returned the kiss.

"All in a day's work, love."

Aunt Butty made a beeline for the side table where Chaz kept his whiskey. He didn't even bat an eyelash as she helped herself.

"We're in a pickle, dear boy," she said between slugs of amber liquid.

"It's true," I admitted when he looked to me for affirmation.

I quickly gave him the run down on everything that had happened since Mr. Singh showed up on my doorstep asking for help. Up to and including the kidnapping, grilling of Molly Malloy, and our attempts to find John Goode.

Chaz whistled. "Our Mr. Singh sure is a mysterious one. Clever fox. How can I help?"

"You know everyone who is anyone in this town," I said. "How about Mr. Goode?"

Chaz rubbed his chin. "Met him once. Dull fellow. Party or some such. Can't recall."

"Do you know where he spends his time of an evening?" Aunt Butty asked, already pouring herself another drink.

"Can't say as I do," Chaz admitted, "but obviously he hangs out with the theater crowd, so I can gander a guess."

"Come along then." I grabbed his sleeve and dragged him toward the door. "Let's go find the man."

"Darling, I'm hardly dressed," he protested. "And neither are you. Go home. Put your glad rags on, and I'll take you on the town. Perhaps Mr. Singh can chauffeur us about. He may recognize this John Goode from his time in the Brighton Hospital."

"Oh! Jolly good idea!" I said. "Isn't it, Aunt Butty?"

"Hmmm? Oh yes. Jolly good indeed." She was already looking more than a little tipsy. How much whiskey had she had?

"Maybe you should stay home, love." Chaz wrestled the glass from Aunt Butty's grip. "Let us do a bit of sleuthing."

"And face danger on your own? Never!" She shot us both glares that were less impactful than they would have been if she hadn't been weaving a bit on her feet.

"How much has she had to drink?" Chaz whispered, unknowingly voicing my own thoughts.

"I didn't think that much," I whispered back. "I mean, she had a couple on the train."

"How many?"

I mulled it over. "Two. No, three. But that's nothing."

"And since?"

"Well, two here."

"She had three."

"Oh." I blinked. Somehow, she'd slipped the third one by me. "But still. Aunt Butty could outdrink a fish. There's no way even six drinks would have such an effect on her."

"What about when you went to Goode's? Did she poke around in his cabinets?"

"Oh, dash it all!" I'd forgotten her habit of filling up her flask from other people's liquor cabinets. "I think she got into his gin. Kept going on about how cheap it was."

He lifted a brow.

"She's right. Cheap as chips. Horrible taste," Aunt Butty said, staggering to the couch and sinking into the cushions.

"Do you suppose there was something in the gin?" I asked Chaz.

"One way to find out," he said grimly. "Hand over your flask, Aunt B."

It took some wrestling, but we finally got it from her. Chaz unscrewed it and gave it a sniff, then a tiny taste. He frowned. "Laudanum. And a lot of it. No wonder the gin tastes off."

I knew laudanum to have a bitter taste. "Will she be alright?"

He shook the flask which was still mostly full. "Fortunately, I don't think she had much. She'll sleep it off."

"I'll call Mr. Singh. He and Simon can take her home where Vera can get her into bed. If she can manage." Vera was possibly the worst maid in the history of maids, but my aunt was fond of her, and surely she could manage this simple task.

While I rang Mr. Singh, Chaz finished dressing. He returned looking the bee's knees. I suddenly felt dowdy in my travel dress which was a bit mussed from our investigations. "I really must get home and change. But I don't want to leave until Mr. Singh collects my aunt."

"He should be here soon enough. In the meantime, I've been thinking about that laudanum."

"Do you think Goode put it in the gin on purpose?"

163

He shook his head. "Doubtful. There's no way he could have known you and your aunt would break in and steal his gin. And there's too much of it to be safe to drink."

I wanted to protest about the whole breaking and stealing thing, but he wasn't wrong. "Do you think someone was trying to murder him?"

"That's the most likely scenario. Question is, who would want to kill a low-level bureaucrat?"

"Maybe for the same reason he kidnapped me. Something in his past," I said.

"Are we sure he was involved in your kidnapping?"

"Well, his car was. I don't know about him in particular. But I was thinking on how the kidnappers could have known we were in Brighton to investigate Emily's death. And the only person who could have known, other than me, Aunt Butty, Simon, and Mr. Singh, was John Goode. He was sitting in the lobby of the hotel while I was on the line with Maddie. I asked her to bring me my things because it was going to take longer than I thought."

"And you definitely told her why you were there?" he asked.

"Yes, of course."

"And he for sure heard you?"

I thought on it. "Pretty sure. He was close enough he could have heard, and he gave me a strange look when I passed him."

"Alright, so he overhead your phone call and knew you were there investigating. So he calls his goons, has you kidnapped to try and get you to drop it. We still don't know why, and it still doesn't lead us to why someone would want to kill him."

I sighed. "No, it doesn't. We need to talk to John Goode as soon as possible!"

We made a quick stop at my house, where I changed faster than I probably had in my entire life. Hale had already left for his gig, so I scribbled a note just in case he returned before I did, and we were on our way to one of the clubs where Chaz assured me the theater crowd hung out.

The club was located in the West End, wedged between an aging theater and a tall building of indiscriminate use. It was narrow but deep with low ceilings, smoky air, loud music, and too many bodies shoved into one space. I began to sweat almost immediately. I know a lady isn't supposed to admit to such a thing, but it's true nonetheless.

After getting drinks—watered down to the point of being fruit juice— from the bar, we huddled together at the edge of the room. There was so much color and movement and bare flesh, it was enough to send a person into a fit.

"What's the plan, old thing?" Chaz asked.

"Let's split up. Ask around about Mr. Goode. Surely someone here knows him. I mean Molly Malloy is his main squeeze, for goodness sake."

Chaz stuck one hand in his trousers pocket and sauntered along next to the bar, occasionally stopping to chat to this person or that. Meanwhile, I edged my way through the press of people on the other side of the room "accidentally" trodding on various feet.

"Oh! I say!" A portly gentleman lifted his monocle and peered at me.

"So sorry!" I said cheerfully. "Such a crush, don't you think?"

"Indeed." His gaze zeroed in on my rather impressive cleavage.

"Do you know a Mr. John Goode?" I asked.

"'Fraid not. Will I do?" He waggled his bushy eyebrows which were in dire need of a trim.

I gave him a pained smile. "'Fraid not. Johnny's the jealous type." And I slipped away before he could do anything other than leer. Which, of course, would have earned him a handbag upside the head, but I was in a hurry and didn't want to get sidetracked.

The next foot belonged to a blousy blonde who was dressed like a twenty-something but was definitely long past fifty. "Watch it, ducks. These shoes weren't cheap." Her pink painted mouth twisted into a frown before smoothing out, as if she remembered frowning gives a person wrinkles.

"Sorry, darling," I said with a giggle as if I were tipsy. As if I could get tipsy on these ghastly drinks. "Such a mad crush, don't you think? I can't find my friend for the life of me."

"Oh, who are you looking for, ducks? I know just about everybody who is anybody." She stuck out her hand. Every finger had a cheap ring on it that glittered in the dim light. "Carole Bardeau."

"Nice to meet you," I said. "Ophelia Trent." I gave her Aunt Butty's current legal last name. Typically, she went by the title of one of her former husbands—the second, or was it the first? —but her last husband had been plain Mr. Trent, so it seemed an easy enough name to co-op. "I'm looking for John Goode."

Her eyes lit up. "Oh, yes, John. I know him. Isn't he a peach? But I thought he was off to Brighton with Molly Malloy. They're an item, you know." She eyed me carefully as if I might combust with rage.

I waved airily. "Oh I know. In fact, my aunt and I ran into them down there. Lovely couple, don't you think? But I could have sworn he said he was headed back to London."

"He might have done, but I haven't seen him," she admitted. "If I do, should I tell him I ran into you?"

"Don't bother yourself," I said. "If I don't catch up with him tonight, I'll ring him up."

Sometime later, Chaz and I met back up near the bar.

"Any luck?" I asked Chaz.

"Ran into one of his cronies. He's at a private club tonight. I got the address."

"Well that's just swell," I said snarkily. "They don't let women into private clubs."

"They'll let me and my good friend, Oscar, in."
Chaz's eyes twinkled.

"Who the deuce is Oscar?" I'd never heard that
name mentioned.

He threw his head back and laughed. "You, darling.
Want to play dress up?"

I'd once seen a picture of Marlene Dietrich in a
men's tuxedo. She'd looked marvelous. Very daring and
oddly feminine. Unfortunately, in my case, we weren't
going for feminine, and I had far more in the hip
department than the lovely Marlene.

I won't go into the humiliating details of having
one's bosoms strapped to one's chest or trying to make one
of Chaz's evening suits look like it was meant to fit me, but
suffice it to say, things were not going well.

"Maybe you should go on your own," I said, staring
at my reflection. It wasn't encouraging. I couldn't get the
trousers fastened properly, and so they sagged alarmingly

low. The shirt hung loosely off the shoulders but strained in the chest. I couldn't even do up the last few buttons.

"Buck up, old thing. We're in this together. Besides, I don't know what Goode looks like. It'll be easier to spot him if you're there."

I sighed heavily. "Fine, but this is simply not going to work." I tugged at the shirt that hung off my shoulders and clung to my stomach.

Chaz snapped his fingers. "I have an idea."

He disappeared into his bedroom and shortly returned with the most garish, out of date evening suit I'd ever seen. It was tan with thick, burgundy stripes and a fat tie to match. Shudder. It also came with a shirt in an appalling shade of ochre.

"It was my uncle's," he said, holding it up. "I borrowed it for a fancy-dress shindig."

"It looks rather... large."

"Well, Uncle Bill was a portly gentleman," he admitted. "But I'm thinking we can make it work."

"Making it work" involved having a pillow strapped to my front before being cinched into Uncle Bill's trousers with a rather worn-out looking belt. I managed to tuck the shirt over that fairly easily, but I was still swimming in the jacket. Chaz pulled out a pile of linen napkins to serve as shoulder pads, which sort of worked.

I glared at my reflection in the mirror. There was nothing glamorous about it. I looked like a lumpy bump. "I look ridiculous."

"That's because we're not finished." Chaz rolled his eyes. "We need to do something about that hair. Maybe we could just stuff it under a hat."

"And when we go inside, I'll have to take it off. Then what?" My hair, being a head of chin-length curls, was not very mannish.

"We could cut it short."

I snorted. "Not on your life."

"I don't suppose you have any short wigs or anything?"

"'Fraid not," I admitted.

"Well, perhaps slicking it back into a queue would work. Very old fashioned, but what can you do?"

"Whatever you must." I didn't love the thought of my hair being pomaded flat but needs must.

So while Chaz handled my hair, I washed the makeup off my face. The result was rather dubious. My face was not nearly plump enough to account for my rather large fake stomach. My bone structure was a bit too refined and my skin too smooth for a man's.

"The lighting will be dim," Chaz assured me, "and they'll be well in their cups by now. Besides which, people see what they expect to see."

"And they expect to see a fat man with poor taste in clothes?"

He ignored my sarcasm. "They expect to see men of the middle classes, likely with creative or bohemian tendencies. That is the sort of person Goode spends his time with. They won't be expecting a woman. Not in their precious inner sanctum."

I sighed. "Very well. I suppose we'd better go now before I call the whole thing off."

Chaz donned his overcoat as it was rather chilly out. I had no overcoat since Chaz's were too small to fit over his uncle's clothes. Although I did borrow one of his hats which was only slightly large on me.

The private club wasn't far from Chaz's digs, and so we decided to walk. Along the way, we discussed our plan which more or less amounted to me looking around for Goode and pointing him out.

"And then what?" I said.

Chaz shrugged. "Play it by ear?"

"I suppose."

Getting into a private club could be varying levels of difficult. Fortunately in this case, the doorman was easily bribed with a five-pound note, and we were soon inside a bar not unlike the previous one. The difference being the only women present were serving girls in outfits which left little to the imagination.

Despite most of the denizens wearing mid-range off-the-rack suits that had simply been altered by a tailor, I didn't exactly blend in. They still aped their betters, wearing dark colors and straight lines. I rather stuck out like a peacock among pigeons.

Everyone turned to gape at me. I kept my shoulders back, head up, and tried to infuse a manliness into my walk, even while I felt one of the napkins sliding out of its place. I did a sort of one shoulder shrugging thing and managed to keep it from sliding further. Meanwhile, Chaz introduced me loudly to everyone as "My friend, Oscar."

I went to get myself a drink, feeling in dire need of something to stiffen my spine, but Chaz quickly drew me away. "Need to keep a level head, love."

"Wonderful." My tone was bone dry.

At last I spotted our quarry in the far corner, chatting to a couple of men who looked to be around his age. And, based on their bearing, I was guessing former military. How interesting. It was too dark to make out their faces, but from the closeness of their bodies, I was betting these men had known each other for some time—and they were definitely up to something.

"Should we confront them?" I murmured. That had been our plan, after all, but suddenly I doubted these men would tell us anything. I had a very bad feeling about them. They looked quite banal. So ordinary. But my stomach turned at the dark expressions on their faces.

"Maybe we should," he said. "Might stir the pot, so to speak. Jar something loose. Though I can tell you're not terribly fond of that idea."

"I just think maybe we should try and eavesdrop on them first," I said.

"How? Their table is in sight of everyone. They would see us coming."

"A distraction, my dear chap. See how either side of their booth is neatly partitioned off with a wooden screen?" The dividers easily reached a good two to three feet above the seated men's heads, allowing the illusion of privacy.

"Of course."

"Well, if you cause a commotion on one side of them, that's where their attention will go. They'll lower their voices and move toward the other side of their booth, away from you. Eventually, when they realize you and your friends don't care a wit for them, they'll raise their voices. Meanwhile, I will have crept around to the other side to listen in. I won't be able to see them, but I should be able to hear something."

"Brilliant!"

And so it would have been if all had gone to plan. But as these things are wont to do, it went awry almost immediately.

Chaz did his part splendidly. Within minutes he had insinuated himself into the group at the table next to Goode's and ordered everyone a round of drinks. A short time later, his table had grown increasingly loud and increasingly drunk, drawing attention of everyone in the place, including John Goode and his compatriots. This gave me the perfect moment to slip around to the empty table on the other side.

I'd nearly made it there, when the napkin chose this very moment to continue its slide to doom. I tried to shrug it back into place again but somehow managed to lose my balance.

A gentleman seated at one of the tables scooted back his chair quite suddenly into my path, and I stumbled straight into him. I went sprawling head first right in front of John Goode. He stared straight at me, and I could tell from his expression that he recognized me. He just wasn't sure where he'd seen me or who I was, but he *knew* me.

And then someone said, "Good gosh!"

And another, "What the devil?"

And finally, "It's a woman!"

I realized by the breeze against my overheated skin that the buttons on Uncle Billy's shirt had burst open on impact and the pillow—along with the piles of napkins— had flopped out and burst across the floor. I now lay sprawled on the dirty floor with my lacy chemise showing, covered in feathers.

Before I could do much more than scramble to my feet, I was surrounded by black uniformed waiters and frog marched toward the door. I managed to turn around and wave for Chaz to stay. Hopefully he knew that meant I wanted him to continue investigating.

"Madame," the butler sniffed as he shoved me out, sans hat or pillow, "this is a *gentlemen's* establishment. *Females* are not allowed."

Before I could protest—females were obviously allowed if they were dressed like floozies—he'd slammed the door in my face. And there I was, standing on the street, wearing men's clothes that were far too big, and drenched from head to foot—for at some time it had started raining in earnest. I heaved a sigh. No cab was going to pick me up in this state, and Chaz was still inside, so I slogged to the red telephone booth on the corner and rang Aunt Butty.

It was Mr. Singh who answered. He asked no questions other than where he should collect me. Within minutes, I was climbing into Aunt Butty's motor.

"You should have called me earlier," Mr. Singh said in the closest he'd ever come to a reproach. "I could have helped."

I sighed. "You'd have stuck out in there like a sore thumb."

"I could have played the part of your manservant."

"It isn't the sort of place where the members have servants," I pointed out.

"Ah. That would have complicated things. But at the very least, you should have kept someone apprised of your location."

"Indeed. I'm sorry I didn't speak to you first, though. Things went a bit awry." I told him about my disastrous attempt at eavesdropping.

I could have sworn I saw his lips twitch. "Perhaps Mr. Chaz will have better luck," he said.

"One can only hope. He certainly can't have worse."

Chapter 12

I stayed up waiting for Chaz to stop by or ring, but it grew increasingly late and, at some point, I nodded off only to be roused by Hale returning from his gig. I vaguely recall him kissing me on the forehead and murmuring something before padding softly away.

I must have dosed off again because I was woken some time later by the ringing of the telephone. I sat up, realizing I'd fallen asleep in my dressing gown in front of the fire in my sitting room. The sofa was surprisingly comfortable. Had I dreamt about Hale coming home?

Maddie appeared looking a bit paler than usual. "Milady, there's a man on the telephone for you."

"Oh, good. Chaz at last!" I rose and strode from the room.

"No, milady. Not Mr. Chaz. It's... I don't know who it is but he..." She twisted her hands together. "He's not very nice."

"Alright then." I scooped up the receiver and said in my most imperious tone, "Yes?"

"Is that Lady Rample?" The voice was gruff, common, and vaguely familiar.

"Indeed. Who is this?"

"Never mind who this is. I've got your boy."

I blinked. My boy? "I'm sorry, but you have made a mistake. I don't have children."

"Don't be stupid," the mystery man snarled. "I mean that one with you in the club last night."

Chaz. Whoever it was knew I was the woman who'd dressed up as a man. But how? It was not John Goode. His voice was smoother, more upper class. But he must somehow know this man for he was the only person who could have guessed it was me. He likely realized who I was once it was revealed I was a woman and had been hauled out.

"Is he alright?" I demanded.

"Right as rain. But he won't stay that way unless you do as I say."

"What do you want?" I snapped.

"I want you to bring whatever you think you've found on the Emily Pearson case to this address." He rattled it off. Thankfully I always kept a pad of paper and a pencil on the telephone table. "Be there by noon today, or he gets the axe."

"That seems a bit dramatic. How do I know you'll keep your word?" My tone was cool, but my heart was racing a mile a minute.

"You don't," he said slyly. "But if you don't come, he's definitely dead." And he rang off.

I stood there a moment, staring at the phone in my hand.

"Milady? Is everything alright?" Maddie whispered.

"No. No it isn't. Maddie," I thrust the receiver at her, "ring Mr. Singh. Tell him I need him immediately."

"Yes, milady. What will you be doing?" She stared at me with big eyes.

I gave her a grim smile as I tightened the sash of my robe. "Preparing for war."

Hale and I met Mr. Singh in a little neighborhood park not far from the address the kidnapper had given me. Mr. Singh had brought with him a briefcase which looked very official.

"What is that?" I asked.

"Documents. You said the kidnapper wanted documents, so I took the liberty of including some." He nodded to the briefcase.

"What are they really?" Hale asked.

On the drive over, I'd caught him up on the details of our case, leaving out some of the more hair-raising moments. I'd tell him later, but for now I didn't want him focused on me and not our mission.

Look at me, calling it a mission. I almost laughed aloud.

"Some of Lady Lucas's old doctor bills and such," Mr. Singh said, referencing my aunt. "Rubbish that needed gotten rid of." He made as close to an expression of distaste as I'd ever seen him give.

I suppressed a grin. How very like Mr. Singh to play dual duty. Not only did he get rid of the rubbish, but they suited a purpose. Instead I said, "What do we do?"

"The priority, of course, is to free Mr. Chaz, but I would also like for you to get them talking. We need to get a confession."

"Isn't that dangerous?" Hale frowned.

I patted his arm. "I can handle myself, but how will that help? Even if we get one, why would the police ever believe us?"

"Because this case is not just full of documents," Mr. Singh said, laying it on the bonnet of my car. He pressed the latches in a certain combination, and a secret compartment popped open. Inside was a strange machine with two reels, not unlike film reels, but smaller.

"Press the handle of the case down like this." He showed me. "It will activate a secret lever and start the recording tape."

"This is a recording device?" I stared at it in wonder. It was so small! It fit right inside the briefcase.

"Indeed. It is a prototype. Not yet on the market. You must get quite close. As close as you can." He closed the briefcase and handed it to me.

I took it from him with some trepidation. "How the deuce did you get your hands on such a thing?"

"You may have friends in high places, my lady, but I know people in rather lower ones."

Had Mr. Singh just made a joke? Surely not.

"Are you certain about this, my lady?" he continued.

"I have to do it, Mr. Singh. You can't. Nor can Hale. It must be me, or Chaz's life will be in danger."

"I am more worried about your life. As, I am sure, are Mr. Chaz and Mr. Hale. I am the one who got you into this mess."

"You asked for help, and I was glad to give it," I said. "I'm not about to give up now in the eleventh hour." I squared my shoulders. "Once more into the breach."

"You, my lady, are the most admirable of women."

"You got that right," Hale muttered.

I threw a look over my shoulder. "Aw, you two are making me blush."

Up the steps I went and into the building as instructed. Taking a deep breath, I rapped on the door.

The door opened to a dark room, a single spotlight shining in the center. I couldn't see who had opened the door, but I could see Chaz, tied to chair, blood dripping from a cut on his forehead. If they'd harmed him—

Instead of showing my ire, I gazed around calmly. "Well, here I am as you asked."

"Step into the light." It was the same voice I'd heard on the phone. It was so familiar, but I couldn't quite place it

Not sure what else to do, I did as instructed. It put me closer to Chaz. He looked a mess, but at least he was still breathing.

"Show yourself," I demanded.

The was a crunching footstep and then a figure stepped into the light. He was a slight man, barely taller than my own five-foot-six, dressed in a suit that was just a tad big. He moved like a soldier, though, with a straight back and shoulders. I recognized his build as one of the men at the club with John Goode. Even more, I realized he was the man who kidnapped me from the hotel in Brighton. The one I thought of as Gravel Voice. *Tha*t was where I'd heard his voice before.

I carefully set the briefcase on the floor and flipped the handle down, activating the recording. The man's eyes flicked to the case, but he didn't move toward it.

"Who are you?" I asked. "What do you want?"

"As I said on the phone, I want the documentation you have on the Emily Pearson murder," Gravel Voice said.

"What do you have to do with her death?" I demanded.

"That is none of your affair. The woman's been dead for years. Let it go."

"Sorry, I can't do that." It was probably all sorts of stupid to tell the man I wouldn't back down, but Mr. Singh was right. We needed a confession. "I'm not going to stop until I find out the truth."

He sighed heavily and removed a gun from his pocket. He pointed it at me. "That's really too bad."

"That's a gun!" I gasped, wanting to make sure it was recorded on the tape.

"How astute." His tone was dry.

"Are you really going to shoot me? You know who I am. The police won't just let this go."

"They won't find you. You'll be at the bottom of the Thames along with your mate here." Gravel Voice waved the barrel at Chaz who still hadn't moved.

I was getting a bit worried. About both of us, to be honest.

"Well, then, you won't mind explaining things."

"Why? You're going to die. It isn't going to matter."

"True," I said lightly, "but I'm the curious sort. If I'm going to get killed by it, like the proverbial cat, then I should at least get some satisfaction before I do. Don't you think?"

He scowled. "You are an irritating woman."

"You're not the first to say so," I admitted, rather proudly. "Now you and John Goode were in on it together, weren't you? Along with that other man with you at the club, I'm betting. Is he the same man who drove the car when you kidnapped me? The one with the scar? I'm betting so."

"You got it all worked out, don't you?"

"Not really. You see, I know John Goode was behind my kidnapping in Brighton. To what? Throw me off the scent?"

Gravel Voice shifted. "We thought a warning was in order. Figured it would scare you off." He snorted. "Fat lot of good that did. Nosey broad."

"Yes, I'm not easily frightened. All right, so that solves that. Although I'm curious. Who played the part of the housekeeper?" I snapped my fingers, recalling the familiar look of the wardrobe mistress. "It was the woman from the theater who played the housekeeper, wasn't it? Who was Mr. Haigh?"

He snorted. "Too clever by half. Mr. Haigh wasn't at all what you think."

Not at all what I thought. Just like I wasn't what they thought when I posed as a man in Uncle Billy's clothes. Molly Malloy's laugh. At the theater. And earlier at the manor house. "Molly Malloy. *She* posed as Haigh. But why? And I still don't know why you had to kill poor Emily. Because you did kill her, the three of you."

"It was an accident," he said stubbornly, not answering my question about Malloy.

"An accident? You drowned her in the pond!" I snapped.

"Not exactly."

"Then what exactly happened?" I demanded.

"John was chasing her, and she fell in. Hit her head. We didn't hold her under, but we didn't help her up either. Figured it solved our problems." The sneering smirk on his face made me queasy.

"What problems?" I persisted.

"You really are a nosy cow, aren't you?"

"Why don't you tell her, Robert?" another voice broke in. "I've a feeling she knows anyway." John Goode stepped into view.

I actually didn't know much of anything, but I wasn't about to admit it. "Where's your third wheel?"

Goode smirked. "Taking care of your man outside. What?" he said at my start. "You didn't think we'd notice? Well, he won't be our problem for much longer. You're going to have lots of company where you're going."

"I'm sure," I said dryly. Actually, what had caused me to start wasn't that they knew about "my man," but that they seemed to think there was only one. "Now, what's this all about? What did Emily see that she wasn't supposed to?" I eyed them carefully, my mind churning. "It was supplies, wasn't it? You were stealing supplies from the hospital and she caught you at it. I believe that's called war profiteering, and it's highly illegal. Why, they'd have shot you for treason!"

"Indeed," Goode said smoothly, "which is why we had to take care of your little nurse. Only she managed to do herself in instead. Very fortuitous."

"But why would you do that? Weren't you all soldiers? You were stealing from your own men!" The idea horrified me.

Goode snorted. "Not my men. We were wasting our resources on a bunch of heathens from the subcontinent when we could have been using them on our own men. Good, Christian, British men!"

Sweet lord above. "So this is all about greed and racism?"

"Why shouldn't we profit?" Robert said. "We were doing all the work. Making all the sacrifices. We deserved something for our efforts."

"You two disgust me," I snapped. "How can you call yourself men?"

"That's really not your problem, is it?" Goode said. "Robert?"

Robert raised the gun, a cold smile on his face. "Hope you've said your prayers."

Chapter 13

I wasn't entirely sure that saying prayers would do me any good. I was rather distraught at the thought that not only was I about to die along with my best friend in the world, but that I hadn't had a chance to say goodbye to Aunt Butty or Hale. Perhaps I could haunt them in the afterlife. Aunt Butty would love that. I wasn't sure what Hale's reaction would be.

Was there time to throw the briefcase at Roberts and knock off his aim? Or perhaps run at him head-on like an insane person? No, he'd shoot me dead, sure and certain.

So I did what any intelligent woman would do. I simultaneously let out a bloodcurdling scream while dropping to the floor like a rag doll. Only blockheads swoon when in danger, but the good thing about men like John Goode and his mate Robert was they always thought women were blockheads.

Fortunately, I am not a blockhead.

My move threw Robert off guard. He swung the gun toward me, shooting at the same time. The shot went wild, and the recoil threw him off balance. At the same time, both men's attention was on me.

Chaz—who'd been faking this whole time apparently—launched himself forward, chair and all, taking Goode—who was closest—to the floor with him. At the very same time, there was a crash, and Mr. Singh came flying through the window like a ninja. Yes, I know. Wrong country, but there you have it. I'd never seen the like.

With a few furious moves, he had Robert unarmed, pressed face down to the wood floor, arms tied behind his back.

Hale was hot on Mr. Singh's heels, facing off with John Goode who had managed to knock Chaz over and climb to his feet. He looked a little stunned, but his face was flushed with fury and he was reaching for his pocket. I did the only thing I could think of. I grabbed the case and swung it. Right between his legs.

Hale's eyes widened. Goode went down in a heap. There may have been tears. His, not mine.

"Where's the other one?" I demanded a little breathlessly.

"What other one?" Hale asked.

"There was a third man at the club," I explained. "And Robert, the one you're sitting on, told me there was another man involved. I think he's the man with the scar that helped kidnap me."

Hale's eyes grew ever wider. "You were kidnapped? Ophelia—"

"He's not here," Chaz said, cutting off Hale's tirade. "He's on his way to Brazil. And could someone please untie me?"

"Oh right." I kicked the case aside, knelt down, and managed to get the knots undone.

Chaz rose to his feet, rubbing his wrists. "Well that was an experience I could have done without."

"Who is the other man? Do you know?" I asked.

He shook his head. "All I know is that they sent him on ahead to the ship with whatever they had left of their ill-gotten gains. They were going to join him once they'd destroyed the evidence and got rid of the witnesses."

"They're awfully trusting for a bunch of traitors and thieves," Hale said. "He could have run off with the dough. Too bad we don't know who it is."

"I do," Mr. Singh said quietly.

Our heads swung toward him and in unison we said, "Who?"

"It's been awhile, but I recognize these men. They spent a great deal of time at the hospital. That one," he pointed at Robert, "was a clerk. He would have had access to all sorts of records and supplies. Goode was also stationed nearby. I recall he was seeing one of the young women who worked at the pharmacy."

"Thus giving them access to anything they wanted," Chaz said grimly.

"Yes," Mr. Singh agreed. "I saw them often together. Along with a third man named Adonicus Fitch. He was the man in charge."

"What the deuce kind of name is that?" Chaz wondered.

"Doesn't matter. We have to get to that ship and stop him." I turned to Mr. Singh. "What did this Fitch look like? Does he have a scar?" I only remembered him vaguely from the club. I'd been so focused on Goode.

"Average height, well build, white-blond hair, cut close. He dresses very neatly. Like a gentleman." Mr. Singh frowned in thought. "His eyes are what mark him, though. Like shards of blue ice. And yes. He has a scar on one cheek."

A man with that coloring shouldn't be too hard to spot. "Can you manage here, Mr. Singh?"

"But of course, my lady. Detective Inspector North is already on his way. Your aunt rang him and explained everything. He might not have believed her, but she got Louise involved."

"Of course she did." I didn't bother pointing out North was now a Detective *Chief* Inspector. It was a lot more fun to annoy the policeman. "Very good, then. You stay here. Chaz, Hale, let's go stop a killer."

"No, I'll stay," Chaz said. "I bashed my leg trying to get away from them. I won't be much good to you. Besides," he slid a look at Mr. Singh, "I think perhaps closure is needed."

Mr. Singh bowed graciously. "Closure would be very much appreciated."

The ship was still there when we arrived, careening onto the dock. We clambered out and charged up the gangplank. A uniformed crewman stopped us.

"Sorry, lady and gents, but the ship's been fully boarded. We're about to cast off. You'll have to go ashore."

"No can do, my good man," Hale said, pushing past. "You've got a murderer on board this ship, and we mean to stop him escaping justice."

"Now wait a minute." The crewman reached out to grab Hale, but I stepped in his way.

"Listen here. I am Ophelia, Lady Rample." I had his immediate attention, so I continued. "Aboard this ship is a man who is not only responsible for the death of an innocent young woman, but for the deaths of hundreds, nay thousands, of soldiers during the war."

The young man paled. "What do you mean?"

"The man's name is Adonicus Fitch, and he and his cronies were war profiteers. They stole medicines from a military hospital so they could resell them, leaving our boys without supplies that were desperately needed."

His face flushed angrily. "I did my duty in that war. I can't abide those that didn't. They deserve to be punished."

"Yes, they do," Hale agreed. "And two of them are already in police custody. The third is aboard this vessel. He will escape if we can't stop him."

"Help us," I pleaded.

The young man nodded. "Digby at your service. What'd you say his name was?"

Hale, Mr. Singh, and I exchanged triumphant looks.

"Fitch," I said.

He flipped through some papers on a clipboard. "Right. This way, please." He stopped only long enough to murmur something to one of his colleagues, and then we were trotting after him through the massive ship. "Where are the police?"

"On their way." I hoped that wasn't a lie. We hadn't taken the time to call them, but I'd no doubt Chaz would tell North about it as soon as he arrived to arrest the other men.

Digby led us across the deck and down a rather narrow set of stairs before knocking on a door. Without waiting for an answer, he swung it open. Inside sat a man with white-blond hair, ice blue eyes, and a scar on his check. It was the driver who'd helped kidnap me. He was in the process of counting stacks of money.

I stepped inside. "Adonicus Fitch, I presume. Counting your ill-gotten gains?"

"How many soldiers had to die for you lot?" Digby sputtered.

"You have no authority over me here," Fitch said with a sly smile. "The ship will leave any moment, and there's nothing you can do about it."

"I say, yes there is!" Digby declared.

Fitch ignored him. "How did you find out about me anyway? Those guys spill their guts? Weaklings."

"I saw you at the club and an old friend of mine told me who you were," I said.

He lifted a brow. "Old friend?"

I smiled coldly. "Remember a young woman you killed? Emily Pearson?"

"We didn't kill her. It was her own fault."

Hale snorted. "Helped along by you."

"Hardly. It was Dorothy that gave her the stuff, not us," Fitch said.

That was a new one. "The stuff?"

"You know, something to make her woozy," Fitch said, standing up. "Dorothy said the stuff would make Emily confused. She'd wander out into traffic or something. It would take care of our little problem."

"The problem of Emily knowing what you were up to," I guessed.

"Sure. We were just supposed to follow along. Make sure she didn't just take a nap on a park bench. Best for everyone she fell into that pond." He laughed.

Mr. Singh let out a sound I'd never heard from him before. A low, almost feral growl. Fortunately, I was standing in front of him so he couldn't get past me to wring Fitch's neck. Although I almost wished he would.

"So it was Dorothy behind all this? The thefts of the hospital's supplies, Emily's death?" I asked.

"She was the mastermind."

"But why?" I demanded.

"Money of course. Woman had ambitions." He said it as if it were perfectly logical.

My gaze never left Fitch's. "There was a young man Emily loved. A man called Mr. Singh. He remembers you." I stepped aside, allowing Fitch to see Mr. Singh.

Fitch ground his teeth. "She deserved to die anyway, cavorting with the likes of him."

"And you deserve to die for what you did!" Mr. Singh snapped, a look that chilled me to the bone washing over his face.

Digby pulled back a fist, ready to strike Fitch in his smug face. I almost wished he would.

"Easy Digby," Hale cautioned.

"Yes, easy Digby," Fitch mocked.

I glanced at the money spread out on the bed in neat little piles. "Let me guess, you had no intention of waiting for your cronies. You planned to take off to Brazil without them and leave them holding the bag."

"More for me, you see." The smile he gave turned my stomach. He stood up and pulled a gun from beneath his jacket and took a step back toward the open balcony door.

"What is with people and guns today?" I groaned.

"I don't know," Hale muttered, "but I'm starting to feel like the only one who's unarmed."

Digby didn't say anything. He just picked up a metal waste bin and threw it at Fitch's head.

The bin hit with a clang. The gun went off. Digby dropped to the floor. And Adonicus Fitch staggered back out onto the balcony and slowly tipped over the rail. Hale and I rushed to the door just in time to see him hit with a splash.

"He's getting away!" Hale shouted.

Only he wasn't. For just at that moment, Mr. Singh swan dived in after him. At the same time, two police cars raced onto the dock, and North popped out shouting instructions. Within seconds, Mr. Singh had got Fitch into a headlock, nearly drowning them both in the process. Shortly after, he dragged Fitch from the water. North clapped the criminal in irons and thrust him in the back of one of the vehicles while we watched, impressed.

Someone handed Mr. Singh a blanket. I waved at him and he gave me a nod, somehow looking elegant even when soaked to the skin, his dastar listing to one side, dripping water.

North stood on the edge of the dock, fists on hips, staring up at me. "Satisfied?" he shouted.

"Very," I called back. "You really do come in handy now and then."

Shéa MacLeod

Chapter 14

It was some hours later before I made it home. There had been questions to answer and money to count and stories to go over. It was all exhausting.

But it was all worth it when Mr. Singh bowed gravely and said, "My lady, I thank you. I am eternally in your debt."

"There are no debts among friends, Mr. Singh," I said. And I meant it. I would have hugged him right there in the police station, but I didn't think he'd appreciate it.

But at last I was home and out of my now rather filthy gown. Maddie hauled it away with a moue. "I'll do my best, milady, but this..." she shook her head.

Shéa MacLeod

Once I was in something more comfortable, I joined Hale and Aunt Butty—who had popped by—in the sitting room where he fixed us drinks before joining me on the sofa near the fire. I felt as if I could breathe easily for the first time in an age.

"I can't believe you were kidnapped," Hale said as he toyed with a lock of my hair.

"Nor can I. It all seems like a surreal dream."

"Why didn't you tell me?"

"I was going to, but then the whole kidnapping thing with Chaz happened and…" I shrugged. "I figured there'd be time later."

"So how did this all work?"

"It was all Dorothy Evans's idea," I said. "She figured out a way to steal medicines and supplies from the Brighton Hospital and resell them with the help of her boyfriend, Goode, and his cronies Fitch and Robert— whose last name is Standish, by the way. Standish got a job as a clerk at the hospital, and Dorothy got herself transferred into the pharmacy. Between them, they stole enough supplies to make a small fortune."

"Is this the same Dorothy Evans who wrote the letter to Mr. Singh?" Aunt Butty asked.

"The very same," I said. "She was the key to helping in their thievery, and she was the one who told them that Emily was on to them. She was also the one who came up with the plan to drug Emily in the hopes she'd get into an accident. Which she did."

"Terrible woman," Aunt Butty said. "I hope they catch her."

I grinned. "Oh, they will. You see, the reason we couldn't find Dorothy Evans isn't because she married and moved to London. It's because she moved to London and became an actress."

Aunt Butty's eyes widened. "Molly Malloy!"

"The very same," I agreed. "She's always been in love with John Goode. When he asked her to help him with the kidnapping stunt, she posed as Mr. Haigh and had the wardrobe mistress, who she's known for years, pose as the housekeeper."

"Well! I never!" Aunt Butty swallowed her cocktail in one go.

With a grin, Hale got up to make her another. "Detective North has them under arrest already, doesn't he?"

"He does."

"And all this time, poor Mr. Singh never knew what happened to the woman he loved," Aunt Butty mused as Hale handed her a fresh cocktail.

"No, he didn't. At least now he knows. Not that it makes it any better." I sighed. There were so many mysteries left about Mr. Singh. I wondered if I'd ever discover the entire truth about him. "I wish... I don't know. I just wonder what he might have been like if Emily had lived. Would they have been happy together? I like to think they would have been."

"Ever the romantic," Hale teased.

"I never thought so before," I admitted, "but yes. Perhaps."

"Well I for one hope we are excitement free for a while," Aunt Butty said. "I could really use a bit of a rest."

"And what would you do with yourself?" I asked, bemused.

"I was thinking running with the bulls sounded relaxing."

The End.

Coming in Fall 2019

Lady Rample and the Haunted Manor

Lady Rample Mysteries - Book Eight

Sign up for updates on Lady Rample:
https://www.subscribepage.com/cozymystery
In the meantime, look for the new cozy mystery series
coming this summer, starting with **A Death in Devon.**

Note from the Author

Thank you for reading. If you enjoyed this book, I'd appreciate it if you'd help others find it so they can enjoy it too.

Lend it: This e-book is lending-enabled, so feel free to share it with your friends, readers' groups, and discussion boards.

Review it: Let other potential readers know what you liked or didn't like about the story.

Sign Up: Join in on the fun on Shéa's email list:
https://www.subscribepage.com/cozymystery
Book updates can be found at www.sheamacleod.com

About Shéa MacLeod

Shéa MacLeod is the author of the bestselling paranormal series, Sunwalker Saga, as well as the award nominated cozy mystery series Viola Roberts Cozy Mysteries. She has dreamed of writing novels since before she could hold a crayon. She totally blames her mother.

She resides in the leafy green hills outside Portland, Oregon where she indulges in her fondness for strong coffee, Ancient Aliens reruns, lemon curd, and dragons. She can usually be found at her desk dreaming of ways to kill people (or vampires). Fictionally speaking, of course.

Other books by Shéa MacLeod

Lady Rample Mysteries
Lady Rample Steps Out
Lady Rample Spies a Clue
Lady Rample and the Silver Screen
Lady Rample Sits In
Lady Rample and the Ghost of Christmas Past
Lady Rample and Cupid's Kiss
Lady Rample and the Mysterious Mr. Singh
Lady Rample and the Haunted Manor (Coming Fall of 2019)

Sugar Martin Vintage Cozy Mysteries
A Death in Devon (Coming Summer 2019)

Viola Roberts Cozy Mysteries
The Corpse in the Cabana
The Stiff in the Study
The Poison in the Pudding
The Body in the Bathtub
The Venom in the Valentine
The Remains in the Rectory
The Death in the Drink

Witchblood Mysteries
Spells and Sigils (Coming August 2019)

Intergalactic Investigations
Infinite Justice
A Rage of Angels

Notting Hill Diaries
Kissing Frogs

Kiss Me, Chloe
Kiss Me, Stupid
Kissing Mr. Darcy

Cupcake Goddess Novelettes
Be Careful What You Wish For
Nothing Tastes As Good
Soulfully Sweet
A Stich in Time

Dragon Wars
Dragon Warrior
Dragon Lord
Dragon Goddess
Green Witch
Dragon Corps
Dragon Mage
Dragon's Angel
Dragon Wars- Three Complete Novels Boxed Set
Dragon Wars 2 – Three Complete Novels Boxed Set

Sunwalker Saga
Kissed by Darkness
Kissed by Fire
Kissed by Smoke
Kissed by Moonlight
Kissed by Ice
Kissed by Blood
Kissed by Destiny

Sunwalker Saga: Soulshifter Trilogy
Fearless
Haunted
Soulshifter

Made in the USA
Las Vegas, NV
25 February 2023

68134772R00125